A
Pawsitively
Purrfect
Match

I0580796

Catnapped

Catnapped

PEPPER MCGRAW

Contents

P
M
G
Publishing

One

BYGUL DESPERATELY NEEDED some time off from Pawsitively Purrfect Matches.

He was the cat companion of a goddess, after all, which made him practically a god himself. He deserved the time off, especially after working so hard on his latest matches.

He planned to make his report, then escape the PPM as soon as possible.

The sun was high overhead and he had grand plans for that bright patch of sunlight he'd seen just a few moments before.

He was almost to Freyja's office door when he realized she wasn't alone.

"I've never known a human in more desperate need of companionship."

Bygul twitched his whiskers and laid his ears back in dismay. That was Bastet's voice. He'd really rather not deal with her today.

"Agreed." And *that* was Ceridwen. Even worse. "Who's available to match her?"

Bygul backed away slowly. He'd come back later, catch Freyja when she was alone.

"Just Bygul," Freyja said.

Bygul froze in mid-step. Well, that was rather rude! He wasn't *just* anyone. He was her cat companion, for goddess' sake!

"Not Bygul." Ceridwen groaned. "He'll make a total mess of things."

Bygul growled low in his throat. He didn't make a mess of anything! His matches were perfect in every way.

"He has the best success record of all our matchmakers and you know it, Ceri," Freyja said.

Exactly! *Thank you, Freyja.* Bygul would have to remember to bring her a special gift next time he visited.

"Yes, but he'll insist on making more than just the companion match."

That's it. Scratch Ceridwen off his Christmas list. No more decapitated birds for her!

"Actually," Freyja said. "The likelihood of him succeeding in this particular case—"

"Practically zero," Bastet said.

What? How insulting! Bygul was the best matchmaker they had on staff!

"Then why are we even having this conversation?" Ceridwen demanded. "We shouldn't waste our resources if she's not a good candidate."

"Oh, she's a perfect candidate for a companion," Freyja said.

"But terrible for a mate," Bastet said. "Which is excellent news for us. If Bygul fails to find her a mate—"

As if!

"He might finally give up his quest to mate-match all of his humans," Freyja said.

"But if he succeeds," Ceridwen wailed, "he'll *never* stop!"

Ceridwen was so melodramatic. And wrong, of course. Nothing would convince him to stop matching his humans, not even failure, a word that had never been associated with *any* of Bygul's matches—and never would be, if he had anything to say about it.

"Trust us," Bastet said. "There's no way he'll succeed with *this* human."

Now, that was just insulting. Bygul was a Norwegian forest cat, for goddess' sake, and they never gave up!

Forget the nap.

Bygul took a moment to mourn that patch of sunlight he'd been looking forward to, then shook it off. In his lifetime, patches of sunlight would come and go, but the matches he made would last forever and this particular match definitely called for the number one matchmaker at PPM.

As far as Maggie Winters was concerned, life was nothing but a series of increasingly annoying events.

Nothing made sense.

Ever.

And people were the worst of all.

She simply didn't get along with any of them, beginning with her parents and continuing with pretty much everyone she'd ever met in her thirty-six years on the planet.

They were just incomprehensible.

Take the woman who'd asked Maggie's opinion at the retail outlet she used to work for. *Used to* being the key words in that sentence.

The woman had asked, point blank, whether the dress made her ass look bigger.

Maggie was simply telling the truth when she said, "Oh, yes, it's quite prominent in that dress, actually."

She had more to say, of course, but the woman didn't appear to be listening as Maggie went on to explain that the dress did a beautiful job of accentuating *all* of the woman's assets, backside included.

Unfortunately, the woman had thrown a fit in middle of the department store and had demanded Maggie's manager fire her on the spot.

Maggie's protests that she was just answering the

woman's question and that it was a compliment in any case went completely unheard.

Maggie really didn't understand why the woman was so upset. Why would she even ask such a question if she didn't want to know the answer?

Even more perplexing was the concept that having a large ass was somehow undesirable. Everyone was built the way they were built and Maggie just didn't understand people's obsession with hiding what made them unique.

It was entirely too confusing.

So that was approximately job number seven hundred fifty-three that Maggie had lost since she began working at age thirteen.

It was the same story over and over again.

Either people didn't appreciate Maggie's honesty or they were assholes.

Or both.

And Maggie frankly didn't put up with assholes.

Like the man who copped a feel when she was serving him a burger and fries.

Or the boss who insisted on calling her sweet cheeks and slapping her ass.

She'd dumped an entire pitcher of iced tea over the head of the first one (job number four hundred ninety-one) and the second, she'd laid out with a single punch (job number one hundred eighty-six).

Overall, Maggie was fine with her rather vagabond, work

lifestyle. She usually had no less than three jobs at any one time because she always knew at least one would be ending imminently. Most of her jobs never even lasted a month and that was fine.

Maggie liked variety.

So far, she'd worked almost every job you could possibly imagine. She'd even worked for a city morgue once upon a time. That had been the perfect job as the only people she ever interacted with, given she worked the nightshift, were dead.

Unfortunately, she discovered she really fucking hated the dead.

They were creepy and disturbing and she kept imagining the zombie apocalypse starting right there in the morgue where she was working. She'd be the first zombie victim and she really wasn't okay with that, especially since she was pretty certain the recently dead would be too hungry to leave any bit of her behind.

This, of course, wasn't what she liked to imagine her role to be in the zombie apocalypse.

At best, Maggie hoped to be a survivor fighting the zombie horde.

At worst, she expected to become a zombie herself.

But entirely consumed by zombies?

No way.

Maggie Winters had no intention of ever becoming the first zombie dinner.

Or would that be breakfast?

Well, it didn't really matter.

The point was Maggie wasn't cut out for working with dead people.

So that was job number three hundred forty-eight, one of the very few she'd quit on her own.

Most jobs Maggie simply endured, at least until she was fired, but keeper of the dead wasn't one of them.

Maggie often wondered, though, if she'd perhaps been too hasty in walking away from that particular job.

After all, the dead weren't anywhere near as annoying as all the living people she'd encountered in her many, varied jobs since.

And so far, as far as she knew, the zombie apocalypse hadn't happened yet, which meant she could have stayed and avoided people and not been eaten by zombies, but she hadn't known that at the time, now had she?

Nor had she realized that most jobs she would be qualified for, as someone blessed with only average intelligence, a GED and a work history that resembled a ping pong ball, would require some form of human interaction, even if only with co-workers and a supervisor.

So there she was, working dead-end, stupid jobs or getting *fired* from dead-end, stupid jobs when something extraordinary happened.

She received a phone call from a lawyer who informed her she'd inherited a small house and some money from a great-aunt she'd never even met.

After much back and forth, as she tried to explain he had

to have found the wrong Maggie Winters because no, she did not have an aunt named Becky, although, yes, she *was* the daughter of Joseph and Sarah, but as far as she knew, her mother had no living relatives at all.

Nevertheless, it appeared Becky did exist and Maggie was her only living heir.

After a rather long conversation that utterly taxed Maggie's patience and communication skills (she had very few, after all), she ended the phone call with a visceral understanding of what people meant when they referred to life-changing events.

Maggie's heretofore unknown aunt was apparently quite well-off or perhaps she simply hoarded her money. Either way, Maggie's life was changed forever.

She couldn't say whether the house or the money was more important. Truthfully, one without the other, wouldn't have provided the freedom they did together.

The money was great, but not so great that Maggie could have purchased a house and had money left over to live on. And while the house was wonderful, without the money, Maggie would have had to continue to work to pay for groceries and utilities.

With both house *and* money, however, Maggie now had the means to retreat from civilization forever.

She would never have to deal with people again!

She'd never have to see that look on their faces when they realized she was serious when she gave them a truth they didn't want to hear.

She'd never have to deal with an asshole boss or an entitled customer or all the tiny misunderstandings that happened day after day when people got all worked up over things Maggie didn't even realize were problems.

Like voting. Why was everyone so worked up about someone getting voted off an island? Maggie didn't even know such a thing was possible. Could anyone be voted off? This island didn't seem a very good place to live if that were the case.

And royal marriages. Why in the world would anyone care about someone else's marriage? Her parents' had been a disaster and Maggie didn't even care about *it*, so why would she worry about the state of a stranger's marriage?

None of it made any sense.

And in a world where nothing made sense, the unexpected gift of being able to retreat from it all was like a dream come true.

So Maggie quit her three jobs. She'd possibly already been fired from one of them, but since she wasn't quite sure about that, she went ahead and quit that one as well.

Her boss looked surprised, so perhaps she really had been fired. Why wouldn't he have just said that though? Maggie couldn't understand why some people never said exactly what they meant.

"I don't think this is the right job for you," wasn't the same as "you're fired," now was it?

She never quite knew how to interpret that statement, so

would always show up for the next shift to see what happened.

Sometimes they came right out and said, "You're fired. Go away."

Sometimes, however, they didn't say anything at all and she got to keep the job. For a while anyway. Until something else happened.

But this unpredictability was why she never really knew.

If "I don't think this is the right job for you" was a synonym for "you're fired," then she shouldn't have been able to continue working at any of those jobs, right?

Only that's not what happened approximately thirty-six percent of the time.

Usually (sixty-four percent of the time to be exact) it *did* mean you were fired, but all those other times, it meant you could keep working if you just showed up.

So that being the case, Maggie always showed up and sometimes she got to keep working.

It was really quite perplexing and yet another reason to be absolutely thrilled to no longer have to work with people.

Maggie actually took quite a bit of pleasure in quitting her jobs.

She didn't even given them notice.

She figured after all the years she'd spent dealing with being fired from job after job with no notice whatsoever, the world owed her the opportunity to do the same back.

So when she quit her final job, the one she was probably

fired from already, but maybe not, she delighted in informing her boss, "I'm sorry, sir, but *you're* fired."

She then walked out, leaving him sputtering in her wake, which was really quite awesome.

A couple hours later, her Honda Civic was packed full of clothes and other essentials and she was ready to hit the road.

Her apartment was on a month-to-month lease so she simply handed her key to the landlord and said, "You can keep the deposit. Use it to get rid of everything I left behind."

"Wait. What?"

She left the landlord sputtering behind her as well, which was also quite delightful. After all, he was just another human being who never said exactly what he meant.

When she first moved in, he'd offered to let her earn her keep in other ways, but everything she suggested, he turned down. She offered to do maintenance, yard work, change lightbulbs, paint the hallways, vacuum the stairs, but he never took her up on any of those offers, and when she demanded to know what he wanted her to do instead, he hemmed and hawed and said to just pay him his rent and get out of his face.

Okay, so maybe he did say what he meant there at the end, but still. She'd wasted so much time trying to think of ways to earn her keep and he never did take her up on any of it. Not even when she offered to run errands for him. Rude.

In any case, that was all behind her now.

No more landlords.

No more bosses.

No more customers.

No more people!

Two

THE FIRST THING Bygul had to do was find the right cat.

According to the PPM's mission statement, this was not a task to be taken lightly. Every cat was unique, after all, and deserved the very best of human companions.

Which was what made this particular matchmaking more challenging than usual. Typically, they started with a cat and then went in search of the perfect human match.

This time, however, a human had come to the attention of PPM and now the task was to find the right cat.

At first, Bygul thought a full-grown cat would be best. One who was big enough for hugging and cuddling. An affectionate cat who wouldn't mind the constant handling.

Then Bygul discovered the human was moving, and more importantly, *where* the human was moving to.

Suddenly, he was on a time crunch.

He had to find the cat and get it bonded with the human *before* she reached her destination. Otherwise, he might not succeed in recruiting a cat to bond with her at all.

Of course, there were *some* cats who would be thrilled at the challenge of living in shifter territory, but they were all a bit crazy, even feral, and possibly not the best match for a woman as lonely as Maggie Winters seemed to be.

In addition, a full-grown cat—especially a feral one—might actually challenge the local shifters, which could result in instant death, a raw deal for both the cat *and* the human.

So perhaps a kitten instead.

After all, shifters were very protective of their young, a protectiveness that might extend to the young of *all* species.

So, Bygul turned his attentions to selecting the perfect kitten companion for Maggie Winters.

Unfortunately, the human was uncooperative in the extreme.

Bygul found three different candidates along the journey toward shifter territory—three!

He placed each of the kittens in the human's path at a different location each time, but did the human do anything Bygul expected in response?

Did she scoop even one of the kittens up into her arms and snuggle him?

Did she carry even one of the kittens home with her?

No, she did not.

Instead, she called the local humane society and

informed them of a kitten abandoned in this parking lot or roaming that park.

Bygul supposed he should be grateful she recruited help for the kittens at all and that she waited until someone showed up to trap them, but all he could really think about was how she left immediately upon the rescue worker's arrival without even a "Goodbye, hope you have a nice life," to the kitten left behind.

This human was most unusual and Bygul was getting desperate.

As the hours passed, she got closer and closer to shifter territory without accepting a single one of the companions he'd specifically chosen for her.

Clearly it was time for new tactics.

Especially when he overheard the human saying to the third candidate, right before she called the Humane Society (again), "Don't look at me with those pathetic little eyes. I'm not the right family for you. You'll find one though, so don't worry. You're cute enough, you'll be adopted right away."

Great.

As much of a risk as it would be to bring a full-grown cat into shifter territory, Bygul was back to thinking this would be the best choice.

So off he went on the hunt for yet another companion for this human who was turning out to be a most difficult human to match indeed.

The human was barely eighty miles from her destination when Bygul finally found the perfect cat.

He was a big, lean tom cat, full of attitude and arrogance.

He'd been in a number of fights over the years. One ear was partially gone and he had a scar and a small, bald spot toward his hindquarters, where something bigger than him had taken a bite.

He wasn't cute and he definitely wasn't adoptable.

He was also quite independent and rather cranky.

He liked living on his own and wasn't exactly looking for companionship, which meant convincing him was no easy task.

It was only when Bygul mentioned living in shifter territory that the cat finally showed a bit of interest, in the form of one good ear perking up.

From there, it was a simple matter of enticing the cat with the promise of endless treats and bright patches of sunlight.

When the cat finally deigned to agree, Bygul transported them both, with seconds to spare, from the alley where he'd found the sad-looking feline to the rest stop along I-70 where Maggie was currently using the restroom.

Bygul hoped this match did the trick because if it didn't, he'd be stuck bringing a slew of cat candidates into shifter territory and *that* had disaster written all over it.

MAGGIE EXITED THE BUILDING AT THE REST STOP and froze.

A giant, raggedy looking gray cat lay stretched across the sidewalk directly in her path.

"For goodness sake!" Maggie set her hands on her hips. "Are these rest stops breeding grounds for cats everywhere?" She looked around, but saw no one who might claim responsibility for this cat. The same thing had happened at the last three stops she'd made.

The only difference was this was a full-grown cat.

One who looked rather the worse for wear.

She inched closer and he didn't move.

He just blinked up at her as if to say, "Well, move around me if you want, but I'm quite content to stay right here."

Maggie crouched down beside him and reached out a hand.

He eyed the hand, but made no aggressive moves, so she gently pet him on the side, then scratched his head, noting one mangled ear and some crusts in his eyes.

"Poor love," she murmured to him. "Has no one been properly caring for you?" She could certainly relate to that.

A rumble started in his chest as she pet him and she couldn't help the tiny thrill of delight that raced through her at the sound.

He was purring!

She really needed to be moving along, but then again, she wasn't exactly on a tight schedule.

She was free.

Free to do whatever she wanted.

No jobs.

No bosses to report to.

No customers to try and please.

It was just her and the open road and the eventual house that had belonged to her aunt Becky, whom she'd never met or even knew existed.

Perhaps her aunt Becky's house needed a cat.

And perhaps this cat needed a house.

Maggie had never considered getting a pet before, mostly because she lived in a series of low-rent apartments that didn't allow for pets, but if she'd ever thought to get one, she'd definitely have chosen a cat.

Maybe even this gray one here.

"Well, then, what do you think? Would you like to come with me? It's your choice. I won't make you." She stood and waited.

The cat let out a rumble, then slowly climbed to its feet.

"Right then." Maggie grinned and led the way to her car. She opened the drivers' side door and the cat jumped inside.

It padded its way across to the passenger seat, where it sat on a mound of clothes and stared out the passenger side window.

Maggie climbed into the car and started it.

She reached to put the car in drive, then hesitated. She really needed to figure out her next steps.

As much as she wanted to get to her new home as soon as possible, she also needed a few things for the cat—a litter box and food, at the very least—and the cat definitely needed medical care.

She looked up the closest vet and headed that way.

It turned out the cat was long overdue to be neutered and those surgeries were only ever scheduled for the morning hours, so Maggie ended up checking them into a motel room for the night.

"I wish I knew your name," she said to the cat as they drove to a local pet store.

Gray Cat was what they'd put on the intake form, but Maggie knew she'd have to come up with something better than that.

She spent an hour at the pet store buying and shoving cat things into the tiny bits of space left in her car, all while the cat watched her from the front passenger seat.

Not once did he attempt to leave the car, which struck her as rather odd, but she was terribly grateful all the same.

Eventually, she carried the cat into their motel room, where she set up a litter box and food and water bowls for him.

He snarfed down the food, then settled on her chest as they watched a documentary series about big cats.

She fell asleep with him curled there, his purr a soft rumble that filled her heart with joy.

Three

WITH THE MATCHING of Maggie to a companion cat, and fairly quickly if he did say so himself, Bygul knew he'd be hearing from the trio goddesses, demanding his immediate return.

He'd ignore them, of course, as no match was complete until he deemed it so.

He'd hold them off by claiming he needed to make sure the cat was adjusting to shifter territory and would be healthy and happy there.

Everyone would know it was just an excuse, of course, but that was okay. Excuses worked.

He'd be using the extra time to match Maggie again, this time to her mate.

Unfortunately, she wasn't cooperative when it came to mate-matching either.

Maggie might have a truly excellent wardrobe and

impeccable fashion sense, catching eyes everywhere she went, but unfortunately, she also had a way of offending people that was truly epic.

The first evidence of this was when they visited the vet, whom Bygul thought might be a good candidate. If not the vet, then perhaps his assistant.

However, neither one seemed to appreciate Maggie's arched eyebrow and acerbic, "That's rather highway robbery, now isn't it?" when paying the bill.

Then he thought perhaps the trucker when they stopped for gas, but Maggie didn't even notice the man was checking her out and before Bygul could somehow manipulate the situation—cause her to trip and fall into the trucker's arms or maybe have the cat escape right in front of the trucker—Maggie was back in her car and driving away and it was too late to arrange anything.

The rest of the trip was spent with Maggie asking the cat over and over again how it felt about this name or that name.

Of course, the cat never had a response in return, though Maggie didn't seem to hold that against him. She seemed to believe that no response meant he didn't approve, which must be why she kept suggesting new names.

Finally, Bygul could take it no longer. "For goddess' sake, just call him Max!"

"Max," Maggie repeated, startling both the cat and Bygul. "What do you think of that name, Mr. Gray Cat?"

The cat, as far as Bygul could tell, had never had a name before and wasn't quite sure what to make of all this naming nonsense. As far as the cat was concerned, he was a cat and that was that.

"I'm not really quite sure about Max. It seems a little common," Maggie told the cat, who simply yawned in response and didn't seem that interested in the conversation at all.

"It's a perfectly good name and he'd be lucky to have it," Bygul snapped. He'd mate-matched a shifter named Max once, quite by accident.

It was a rather convoluted story. He'd been trying to match a cat with a human and a couple bear shifters in the area kept scaring the cat away, so he'd made the shifters go away, sent them on a new quest.

Who knew they'd end up on the other side of the country, opening a Shenanigans right in between cougar and wolf territories, and that one of the bears would mate a wolf named Max?

He hadn't even been *trying* and he'd managed to set into motion a sequence of events that had not only resulted in the matching of a cat companion with a human, but also the mate-matching of not just the one bear and one wolf, but eventually the other bear with *his* mate plus a whole slew of paranormal matings after that.

That was when Bygul decided he was a matchmaking genius who needed to get serious about expanding beyond just matching companion cats to their human counterparts.

Thus he added mate-matching to his services.

His humans were always quite grateful, though the

goddesses didn't exactly appreciate his initiative and the other matchmakers thought he'd lost sight of the mission.

He knew the mission, he just knew his cats would be happier if their companions were happy too.

Happily Furever After — wasn't that what they guaranteed? He was pretty sure it was.

"I'm just not feeling Max," Maggie said. "And since you don't seem to love it either, Mr. Gray Cat, I think we need some help."

"For heaven's sake, woman!" Bygul exclaimed. "Just call him Cat then!"

"Cat's not a name. Nor is Gray Cat, nor is even Mr. Gray Cat. We need something better than that."

How the human was even hearing him, Bygul had no idea, especially since he was only visible to the cat population and she didn't seem to realize someone was talking in the first place.

This Maggie woman was the strangest human he'd ever tried to match and he'd had a few really strange matches in his time.

"You look like you've been in a few battles there, my friend," Maggie said to the cat. "So I'm thinking we need a warrior's name. It's really unfortunate the vet confirmed you're a boy. I kind of wanted to call you Bastet."

Bygul choked and almost hacked up a fur ball.

What a wonderful idea!

How he'd missed this opportunity in the past, he had no idea.

Why, he could encourage all his humans to name their companion-cats after the gods and goddesses. Imagine the uproar!

"Catphrodite would be hilarious," Maggie continued. "Or maybe Cleocatra."

Bygul was laughing so hard, he almost fell off the dash where he'd settled early in the trip. He was completely shielded from human sight, but the cat could see him and kept an eye on him the entire time.

"Actually, I don't see why I can't go ahead and give you a girl's name," Maggie said. "We could push those gender barriers, right?"

The cat lurched to his feet and hunched over, beginning to gag.

"Oh, no, don't hack up a furball in here!" Bygul exclaimed. "She might decide you're more trouble than you're worth."

"Okay, okay," Maggie said. "I guess Purrsephone's out of the question. Settle down. I'll come up with a boy's name for you soon enough."

With a satisfied air, the cat walked in a circle, kneaded the chair a moment, then flopped back onto his side, a smug look on his face.

"You're not as dumb as you look," Bygul informed him. "Nice job."

"I've got it," Maggie announced. "And just in time because I think we're here."

Bygul looked out the windshield and saw that they'd

pulled up to a large farmhouse in the middle of nowhere with no neighbors in sight.

"Come along, Genghis Khat." Maggie turned off the car and scooped the cat into her arms. "Let's go explore our new home!"

THE HOUSE SEEMED TO BE IN PRETTY GOOD SHAPE.

Maggie walked up onto the porch and found the keys under the doormat, just where the lawyer had said they'd be. It seemed a little trusting to leave keys under the doormat, but Maggie wasn't going to complain, especially since it meant she didn't have to socialize.

The first day in their new home Maggie spent cleaning and unpacking.

The second day she did a lot of online shopping, arranging for Amazon to deliver everything from canned goods to a cat tree. She then went exploring.

The third day, she had an appointment with her aunt's lawyer, a Mr. Wilson, to get all the paperwork signed and to take final possession of her inheritance.

The worst part of that entire experience was having to actually talk to people. First his assistant, who looked rather surprised to see her, then the lawyer himself, who looked utterly stunned.

She had no idea why. She'd told him she'd never met her aunt, so she couldn't imagine why he seemed so surprised.

Mr. Wilson asked a couple questions about her parents and where she'd grown up and where she'd gone to school and seemed a little disturbed at her answers.

He asked if she was planning to stay or to sell the house and he seemed even more disturbed when she said she'd be staying. He seemed to feel it would be better for her to go, but that wasn't happening. "I'm good here and that's that," she told him and he nodded, though the look on his face said he did not agree with her decision.

Why it mattered, she had no idea.

He then asked if she planned to look for a job in town and she said, "Absolutely not."

He looked relieved at that—weird—then asked if she already had a job.

At this point, Maggie was done with the entire conversation so she just stared at him.

He waited for her to answer and she waited for him to realize she wasn't going to.

The silence stretched on long enough that Maggie wondered if it was an awkward silence. It didn't seem awkward to her, but she'd come to realize over the years that her definition of awkward was not everyone's else's.

Silence didn't bother Maggie, but wasting her time did, so she eventually broke the silence by asking, "Are we done here?"

A look of surprise flashed across Mr. Wilson's face—

again—but he just nodded and said, "We are. Good luck with everything."

Maggie, though, was already striding out the door, quite relieved to have this last bit of required socializing behind her.

She was famished after the meeting and desperately needed food. She really wanted to just go home, but wasn't looking forward to yet another dinner made up of canned green beans.

Unfortunately, her only other options were to eat out somewhere, which would involve dealing with people, or to go grocery shopping, which would also mean dealing with people.

However, if she went grocery shopping, she'd have more options than green beans for tomorrow's meals as well.

She'd been severely disappointed when she'd discovered the town of Greensboro only had one grocery store and they did *not* deliver. She'd already found a meal subscription service and had placed her first order, but it wouldn't arrive for another week and she'd never survive that long on green beans.

So, though she dreaded it, grocery shopping it was.

She hurried through the grocery store, avoiding people and trying not to notice as they stopped and stared every time she came near. It had to be because it was such a small town. They probably didn't get many strangers here, that was all.

Still it was unnerving and by the time the cashier had

finished ringing up her groceries, Maggie was exhausted, especially since the woman insisted on asking invasive questions.

"Why are you here?"

"How did you find us?"

"Where are you staying?"

Maggie really wasn't in the mood to answer any of the cashier's questions, which meant her responses became increasingly curt as time went on.

"To get groceries."

"You're on a public street."

"None of your business."

It was the last reply that finally stopped the litany of questions.

Maggie paid and helped bag the last of her groceries. She then grabbed the bags and muttered, "Have a nice day," before hurrying out of the store.

She didn't even know why she'd added that bit at the end.

She certainly didn't *care* whether the nosy cashier had a good day or not, which meant that Maggie was guilty of the one thing she hated the most. She'd said what she didn't mean.

Because what she really meant was, "Don't ever talk to me again."

Maggie hurried to her car, slung the groceries inside and raced home.

When she walked inside, Genghis Khat greeted her with

a symphony of meows and wound himself around her ankles, making her smile.

"Yes, I know, I'll never leave again, how's that?" She began putting the groceries away, all the while talking to the cat about the snippy assistant, the disapproving attorney *and* the nosy cashier. "We have enough groceries to last until I manage to get my meal subscriptions delivered. So we should be fine, Genghis Khat. Just fine!" With that, Maggie retreated to the very comfortable recliner in the living room.

Genghis Khat settled on her lap and they spent the evening together, Maggie reading a stream of books on her Kindle and Genghis Khat snoozing and purring on her lap.

Four

I
T WAS UNFORTUNATE, but Bygul was beginning to think the goddesses might have been correct. The horror of it all!

This particular match was practically impossible.

As it turned out, Bygul was increasingly impressed with the fact he'd managed to match Maggie with a cat at all. She'd truly fallen in love with Genghis Khat, which Bygul now considered to be a minor miracle seeing as the woman was a recluse the likes of which Bygul had never seen before.

In four weeks, she hadn't returned to town, not even once.

The woman did leave the house to work in the yard, to do some gardening and to go on early morning strolls along the deserted stretch of road that led to town. However, she always turned back before reaching any signs of civilization.

Genghis Khat accompanied her on these walks and serenaded her from the screened porch when she worked in the backyard and from the bay window when she worked in the front.

In other words, the only contact the woman had had with another living being was the cat. She hadn't spoken to a single human since that disastrous trip into town.

Bygul had hoped perhaps to set her up with the attorney, but he'd been entirely too old and had clearly disapproved of Maggie. Probably because she wasn't a shifter, which was definitely a bit of a wrench in the works.

He'd then hoped she'd meet someone at the grocery store, but everyone there had given her a wide berth and she'd been epically grouchy with the cashier, potentially solidifying a reputation that was already on shaky grounds due to being human.

After a week of no progress, the goddesses had demanded Bygul turn his attention to matching a feral cat in desperate need of a home. As a result, he'd had to put his attempts to mate-match Maggie on hold while attending to other business.

Over the following three weeks, he'd popped in every once in a while just to check on her progress. He'd hoped in his absence she'd simply gravitate toward her mate the way the wolf and the bear had gravitated toward each other.

Unfortunately, Maggie was, as usual, completely unco-operative.

According to Genghis Khat, she'd sworn off human interaction entirely.

Bygul wondered whether she would change her mind if she knew the humans in town could all shift into animals.

Probably not.

She seemed a stubborn sort.

Unfortunately, Bygul couldn't stick around to force the issue as he had many humans to find for the cats on his matchmaking list. This meant he needed to recruit some help and the only candidate for that was Genghis Khat himself.

Genghis Khat, much like his human, wasn't super cooperative at first—more evidence that Bygul was an excellent matchmaker—but then Bygul reminded him that the town was full of shifters.

Of course, a cat with one mangled ear, scars along his backside and a name like Genghis Khat would perk up at the thought of tangling with some shifters who in shifted form were approximately ten times his size.

The trick was to somehow get the woman to meet the many eligible shifters in town, and as far as Bygul was concerned, the cat was the key.

Maggie was one month into her new life and she absolutely adored it.

She loved living so far out, there were no sounds of any neighbors.

She loved her aunt's house and the garden and the cat most of all.

She loved having enough time in the mornings to really think about what she wanted to wear and what items would look amazing together.

Okay, so no one ever saw her fantastic fashion sense, but she didn't really care. She modeled her clothes for Genghis Khat and absolutely loved that as well.

Who knew that one not-so-small and not-so-pretty cat would become so important to her happiness in such a short amount of time?

Genghis Khat followed her throughout the house, moving from room to room and listening to her ramble about whatever she wanted to talk about on any particular day.

He rarely responded, though he *did* have quite a strong meow, which she was treated to the first time she left him behind to go on a walk without him.

After that, she ordered a harness and leash from Amazon and though Genghis Khat was *not* a fan of either one, he did enjoy their walks outside and thus tolerated them both.

He woke her every morning by patting her on the cheek and on one memorable occasion, biting her on the nose. After that, she made sure to respond by the third pat as she rather liked her nose where it was.

So it was with trepidation that Maggie woke one morning without the usual paw and kitty breath in her face.

She got up and dressed swiftly and went in search of Genghis Khat.

Only he was nowhere to be found.

Literally nowhere.

He'd gone to bed with her the night before and all the windows and doors had been locked. Yet, when she woke the next morning, the window in her study was wide open and Genghis Khat was long gone.

Most disturbing, however, was the one footprint right outside her study window, in the middle of her flower bed.

Someone had broken into her house and catnapped Genghis Khat!

JACKSON HEWITT LOVED HIS JOB, BUT THERE WERE some days it just didn't pay to get out of bed.

Most days, as sheriff of an entirely shifter town, his days were busy.

Between the cougars always riling up the bears and the full moon making the wolves act like idiots, his job as peace-keeper was never dull.

The night before had been rather eventful, with two bar fights in the span of as many hours, so every one of the jail cells at the station were full of belligerent, angry, hungover idiots.

Nine times out of ten, those idiots were men, but on this particular occasion, *three* were women.

The Donnelly sisters. They were an utter pain in his ass and he *lived* for the day they found their mates and became someone else's problem.

For now, they were the problem of the very angry wolf facing him.

"I can't believe you locked up my sisters, Hewitt!" Mark Donnelly growled. "You should have called me."

"Now why would I do that?" Jackson demanded. "Your sisters were each told they could make one phone call and not one of them took me up on the offer. I figured they preferred to just sleep it off."

"You shouldn't have arrested them in the first place!"

"Have you talked to Steve this morning? Because I'm telling you right now, I may have saved your sisters' lives by locking them up."

Mark growled. "That bastard. What's *he* got to be pissed about?"

"It's his bar they destroyed!"

Mark gave Jackson a skeptical look.

"Fine," Jackson sighed. "Their actions incited a fight that destroyed the bar."

"So you arrested them because some assholes got into a fight?"

"No, I arrested your sisters because they were belligerent with my officers *and* they caused the damn fight."

"Sheriff, I'm sorry to interrupt." Connie poked her head

through the door, demonstrating once again that she had epically perfect timing.

"No problem, Connie. Mark, go talk to Danny. Tell him I said to let your sisters go."

Mark let out a huff, turned on his heel and stormed out.

"What's up, Connie?"

"There's a woman on the phone. She's crying and saying her kid's been catnapped."

"What?" Jackson leapt to his feet and grabbed at the phone. He stabbed the light indicating a call on hold and said, "This is Sheriff Hewitt. How can I help you?"

"Sheriff, my name's Maggie. My cat's been taken."

"Right. I need some details from you. Name, age, description."

"Okay. Um. His name is Genghis Khat. I don't know how old he is. Old enough to have gotten into a lot of cat fights. Let's see. Description. He's gray and he's got a mangled ear and he's missing some fur, probably because of those cat fights, right at the tail area. If you see him, you'll know him right off. You can't miss the mangled ear."

Jackson had a pencil in hand, ready to take notes, but he only got as far as Genghis before his brain caught up and he realized what he was hearing.

"Hold on, lady. Let me get this straight. You're calling about your pet cat?" He could hear the incredulity in his own voice.

"Yes! He's been catnapped and I need you to come out

and dust for fingerprints and–and–and catch whoever took him.”

“Okay, ma’am, why do you think someone took the cat?”

“Because when I went to bed the doors and windows were all locked, but now the study window’s open and there’s a footprint in the flowerbed right under the window and my cat is missing!”

“Listen, ma’am, the thing is, we’re the police. We help with — um — human problems.”

“Well, I’m a human and I have a problem, so please help me!”

“One moment, ma’am.” Jackson put the crazy woman on hold and banged his head on the desk.

“I take it the cat’s not a shifter,” Connie said, a wealth of humor in her voice.

Jackson glared up at her. “Did you know she was talking about a freaking pet?”

“I had no idea,” Connie laughed. “I just heard catnapped and came running.”

Jackson nodded. “All right. Damn. When Danny’s finished with Mark, send him in here please. We’ll let him deal with the missing pet report.”

Connie snorted. “That’s just mean. Are you *ever* going to forgive him for backing into Miss Maura’s mailbox?”

“Are you kidding me? I had to listen to her complaining for an hour and then I’m the one who had to replace the damn mailbox because she refused to let Danny back on her property and said she wouldn’t trust any of the other deputies either. And then I had to endure her litany of complaints about her body aches and pains and the horror of getting old—old, my ass—the entire time I was out there installing her new mailbox. So no, there is no forgiveness here. Danny gets the shit jobs for the rest of his career. The end."

Connie laughed, "Right. Well, can't say I blame you there." Still laughing, she headed back out to her desk, calling over her shoulder, "Your crazy cat lady's still on hold."

"Damn."

MAGGIE WAS *NOT* A HAPPY CAMPER. THE SHERIFF seemed to take her seriously enough. He told her a deputy would be out right away to help her find Genghis Khat, but then it turned out the deputy was a bit of an idiot.

"Well, ma'am, there really aren't any clues as to where the cat's been taken. I don't rightly know what you expect me to do."

"Dust for fingerprints! Make a cast of the shoe print. Why am I telling you how to do your job? Just find my cat!"

The deputy, who had introduced himself as Danny Morris, gave a big sigh.

"Fine, ma'am. I'll dust for fingerprints, but it's doubtful the catnapper left any behind. Truthfully, if someone was feeling peckish and stole your cat, well, the cat's probably a goner."

Maggie gasped, then screeched, "What?"

Danny winced. "Well, you know, ma'am. I mean, it is the countryside and—and there's a lot of wildlife around and—"

"I'm quite sure the local cougars didn't open my damn window themselves!" Maggie snapped. What was wrong with this man?

At that moment, her cell phone rang in her pocket, making them both jump.

Maggie pulled out the phone and answered, "Hello?"

"Maggie, this is Sheriff Hewitt."

"Yes, Sheriff."

"I may have some good news for you. The owner of the diner just called and said a gray cat sneaked in with one of the customers and has made himself at home."

"Someone took my cat all the way into town, to the diner? But why?"

The sheriff cleared his throat. "Yes, well, I'm not quite sure that's what happened, but you might want to get over to the diner to collect your cat."

"Oh, but couldn't you bring it out to me or–or maybe Danny could collect the cat for me?"

"Ma'am, we are not a taxi service nor are we a pet rescue. If you want your cat back, I'd suggest you go pick him up. I'd also suggest you hurry. You never know in this town. People have all kinds of strange appetites." With that, he hung up on her.

"What the hell does that mean?" Maggie shrieked, staring at the phone.

Danny shuffled his feet. "Um. What's that, ma'am?"

Maggie rolled her eyes. She was starting to hate that word—ma'am. "Apparently my cat's shown up at the diner. Would you be able to go get him for me?"

Danny shook his head and backed up. "Oh no, ma'am. I need to get back to work now." He hurried toward his patrol car.

"Hey, wait! Aren't you going to dust for fingerprints?"

"Nah, that'd be a waste of time, especially now that you've found your cat and all. Have a good day, ma'am." With that, he climbed into his car and drove away.

"Damnit." Maggie couldn't believe she was going to have to go into town. She glanced down at her phone. And right at lunchtime! This was a nightmare. She hurried into the house, grabbed her keys, locked everything up and climbed into her car.

"Just in and out," she muttered to herself as she set off for town. "You don't have to talk to anyone. Just grab Genghis Khat and go."

Five

"THIS CAT IS either the bravest or the stupidest cat I've ever met," announced one of the humans Genghis Khat had followed into the diner.

"You've got that right, George," the waitress said as a murmur of agreement rolled through the diner.

Genghis Khat thought it perfectly obviously that he was *brave* not stupid, but since humans never understood his meows, he didn't bother to correct them. Instead, he continued making his way through the customers, giving each one a solid sniff.

Some smelled better than others, but they *all* smelled wild and Genghis Khat like that. An awful lot.

He was wilder than they were, of course, but for now he was too busy enjoying the tiny bits of meat and other morsels falling to the floor to impress them with his wildness.

Perhaps later.

As he wandered under the tables and accepted the occasional scratch on the head, he listened to the conversations happening above him.

"Where do you think he came from?" someone asked.

"The sheriff said a woman named Maggie's looking for him," the cook called form the kitchen. "She lives out on Cutter Lane."

"Becky's niece, Maggie?"

"I didn't know Becky had a niece."

"Nobody did. I only know because I handled her affairs after she died. Even then, I had no idea her niece was human." This must be the attorney Maggie was going on and on about, the one who disapproved of her staying.

"Becky's niece is human?"

"There's a human living in town?"

"That must be the woman I saw grocery shopping a while back. She wasn't very friendly. Poor Lindsay kept asking questions and the human refused to answer any of them."

"Well, good for her. Lindsay's a busybody." Lindsay must be the cashier Maggie had told him about.

"She was just curious about the human."

"Still."

"I can't believe we have a human in town."

"How long's she been here anyway?"

"It's been at least a month." That was the attorney's voice again.

"I'm surprised we haven't seen her in town more often."

"Do you think she's someone's mate?"

Genghis Khat perked up at the question.

"I hadn't thought of that." The attorney again. "I was so worried about a human moving to town, it didn't occur to me that mate magic could be in play."

"Well, if she's not a mate, something will pull her away. It always does."

"Surprised it hasn't happened yet if she's been here a month."

"Yeah, by now they've usually moved on or found their mate."

"Well, I'm sure the magic will kick in soon enough and she'll be gone."

Interesting.

Genghis Khat had decided he liked this town.

He liked their house and he liked the scent of all these people.

But if there was magic that would send them away from this town if Maggie didn't find a mate here, they were in serious trouble.

The woman hated people, which was why Bygul's mate-matching plan was surely destined for failure.

Genghis Khat had only agreed to help because Bygul kept talking about people shifting into animals and Genghis Khat was curious to meet these peculiar humans.

He knew Bygul wanted him to somehow get Maggie to interact with as many people in town as possible, but he'd really only planned to laze about and wait for her to pick him up and take him home.

Unfortunately, it sounded like he might have to actually be proactive when it came to the mate-matching efforts, if he didn't want to have to move again.

The thought was really quite horrifying.

Genghis Khat, fiercest feral from the streets of Chicago, was now reduced to mate-matching.

"You can do this," Maggie coached herself as she pulled into the parking lot at the town's diner. "No one will be watching. No one is *ever* watching you, not even when you're convinced they are. Just control the crazy, batten down the paranoia and get in and out, preferably without interacting with anyone. In and out. That's it. You can do this."

Dragging in a deep breath, she locked the car and strode toward the door to the diner. "You used to do this every day. You've worked in hundreds of restaurants and stores and dealt with all kinds of people. You can handle five minutes in this diner."

Except, honestly, Maggie wasn't sure she could.

She stopped halfway up the sidewalk, swung around and paced back toward her car.

The past four weeks had ruined her! She'd been working since she was thirteen and had rarely had more than three days off in a row until her unknown aunt Becky changed her life.

Four weeks without having to interact with people had been an incredible blessing, but now she was completely out of practice!

She no longer knew how to talk to people.

No, that wasn't right. Of course, she knew how to talk to people. She'd been doing it her entire life. Just because people didn't like what she said didn't mean she didn't know how to talk to them.

"You can do this, Maggie." She glanced down at the sassy skirt and sleeveless blouse she was wearing and gave thanks that she'd chosen this outfit for today. "You can do this, Maggie," she repeated to herself, "and even better, you'll look fantastic while doing it."

"THERE'S A CRAZY WOMAN ON THE SIDEWALK," Paul Davis reported from where he was sitting by the window. "I'm betting it's the human."

Annie rolled her eyes as she delivered drinks to the table

across from his booth. "Could you be any more of a bigot, Paul?"

"What?"

"You're saying just because she's human, she's also crazy?"

"Noooo. I'm saying she's crazy because she's talking to herself, pacing back and forth and waving her arms in the air."

By this time, a number of people were crowded around the windows staring out at the human, who Annie saw, really did appear to be having an entire conversation with herself.

In public.

"Maybe she's on the phone," Livi suggested.

"I don't see any earbuds," Tom said.

"Maybe they're just really small," Erica said.

"Not seeing any wires," Adam said.

"Maybe they're wireless," Annie said.

"And maybe she's just crazy," Paul said.

Annie threw her arms in the air. "Whatever. Just get away from the windows before you scare the human away." She shooed them all back to their tables. "She probably saw you and that's why she's freaking out. Act normal for goodness' sake!"

"Normal?" Bud called from the kitchen. "What's normal about this town and these people?"

That was a good question. "Fine!" Annie snapped. "Just

don't act like shifters. No sniffing the human and no growling!"

Paul groaned. "Having a human in town is going to be a real pain in the ass."

ALL MAGGIE HAD MANAGED TO ACCOMPLISH WITH that pep talk was to freak herself out even more.

Time to just grab that bull by the horns and get it over with.

She barreled into the diner, then skidded to a stop.

They were *definitely* staring at her.

All of them.

It wasn't her paranoia this time.

She knew it, she knew it, she knew it.

They weren't just staring with their eyes, they were staring with their bodies too!

Some of them had turned clean around in their chair so their bodies were pointed at the door where Maggie was standing.

"Not cool, not cool, not cool," she muttered under her breath. "Just grab the bull by the horns, just grab the bull by the horns, just grab the bull—"

"What bull you talking about there, Maggie?" Mr. Wilson called from across the diner.

"Yeah, there aren't any bulls in here," a man in a booth by the window informed her. "No bulls in town, in fact."

"Paul, knock it off." A woman walked up to Maggie and handed her a menu. "Come along, dear, let's get you a table." She grabbed Maggie's arm and started to pull her through the dining room.

"Oh–oh–oh, no. I don't—I—I'm not—hungry or–or thirsty. I just—I need—"

"Oh, hon. You have to eat a good meal in the middle of the day if you want to keep up your energy. Now what are you in the mood for? Burger and fries, turkey club, fish and chips, meatloaf—"

It appeared the woman was ready to recite the entire menu, so Maggie cut her off. "A turkey club will be fine."

"With the bacon?"

"Sure."

"Fries?"

"Sure."

"What'll you have to drink?"

"Um, I—" Maggie caught sight of a gray blob on the floor under the table next to her and lunged out of the booth. "Genghis Khat!" She landed on her knees beside the table, crawled beneath it and scooped her cat into her arms, thrilled he was safe.

Genghis Khat started to purr the minute she held him close and she slowly backed out from under the table, realizing as she did so, that there were several pairs of legs also under the table with her.

Oh, well.

Most people would apologize, but Maggie didn't believe in apologizing for things you weren't sorry for and she'd have crawled under a hundred tables to rescue her cat again.

She settled back in the booth with Genghis Khat in her arms and set him on the table in front of her. "Oh, Genghis Khat, I was so worried," she whispered to him. "You have to tell me who catnapped you." She sent a narrow-eyed glare around the room, noting that *everyone* in the room was *still* staring at her.

In fact, even though she was now on the opposite side of the room from the door, everyone had swiveled around so that their bodies were now turned her way again.

She looked back at Genghis Khat, who flopped onto his side and let out a huge yawn. "Seriously?" she whispered. "It wasn't anyone in the diner?"

She cast another suspicious look at the diners.

No one looked guilty, though they all seemed somewhat surprised. Or disturbed. Or something, she wasn't quite sure what.

But guilty?

No.

"This doesn't make any sense, Genghis Khat. Why would someone break into our house and catnap you, only to drop you off at the diner in town?"

The sound of a throat clearing interrupted Maggie's train of thought, bringing her attention back to the waitress, whose name according to the tag on her shirt was Annie. "Oh. You're still here?"

"Waiting for your drink order, hon."

"Oh, right, uh, coke for me please and maybe a bit of milk for Genghis Khat?"

Annie smiled. "You got it."

Maggie waited until the waitress was out of earshot, then turned back to Genghis Khat. "Nothing to say, eh? I assume that means your catnapper's long gone."

Genghis Khat wasn't the greatest of communicators, but Maggie was still pretty sure he'd implicate the person responsible if they were still in the diner, so Maggie mentally crossed everyone present off her suspect list.

Unfortunately, since Maggie's list only consisted of the people currently inside the diner, there was no longer anyone on it.

"You're the best cat ever. If I'd catnapped you, I'd never let you out of my sight. I certainly wouldn't leave you behind at a diner full of strangers. I can't imagine why your catnapper abandoned you. Unless—did you *escape*, Genghis Khat?"

He nudged Maggie's hand.

"Sorry, sorry, didn't mean to stop petting you." Maggie scratched his head and began to stroke him again.

"I bet you did escape. You're so smart, but you know what that means? It means the catnapper's still out there and he may come back for you later. I'd call the sheriff, but I have to tell you, I'm not that impressed with his deputy, and the sheriff seemed a bit unwilling to handle it himself. That's okay, though. We can handle a catnapper between the two of us, right?"

"Here you go. One turkey club and fries, one coke and one saucer of milk." Annie set each item on the table as she announced it.

In addition to not apologizing for things she wasn't sorry for, Maggie didn't believe in saying thank you for things she wasn't actually grateful for. She just didn't understand false gratitude, and as a result, hadn't been planning to thank Annie since she hadn't wanted food in the first place.

However, when Annie settled the plate in front of Maggie and she inhaled the delicious scents of the turkey club and fries, she realized she was quite hungry, and therefore, grateful after all. "Thanks, Annie."

Without waiting for a response, she carefully peeled apart the sandwich, removed two slices of turkey from its center and reassembled it. She then began to methodically tear the turkey into tiny bite-size pieces for Genghis Khat, who was busy lapping up the milk.

"So." Annie plopped into the seat across from Maggie, startling her and Genghis Khat, who let out a soft hiss of surprise.

"It's okay, sweetheart." Maggie stroked her hand down his back and he went back to lapping up the milk.

"What's your name?" Annie asked.

"Oh, um, Maggie."

"Nice to meet you. I'm Annie. My parents own the diner."

Maggie nodded. She had no idea what to say in response. Was she even expected to reply?

Annie hadn't asked a question so Maggie wasn't sure.

Maybe Maggie was supposed to share about her own parents, but she didn't want to, so she didn't.

Once again, as the silence stretched out, Maggie wondered if it was becoming awkward.

Since Maggie loved silence, she wasn't sure how long it had to last before it became awkward for others.

In truth, Maggie thought silence was a beautiful thing.

She could sit in silence all day long, even when surrounded by people, even if none of them spoke a word to her. In fact, she'd prefer that.

However, she knew from countless prior conversations that most people were uncomfortable with silence.

She waited to see if Annie was one of those people.

If she was, she'd either make an excuse and rush away or she'd break the silence by asking a question, thus forcing Maggie to participate in the conversation.

The silence stretched long enough that Maggie managed to finish tearing apart both slices of turkey and to cut her sandwich into fourths.

Without looking up, Maggie ate one-fourth of her sandwich with her left hand, while feeding tiny bits of turkey to Genghis Khat with her right.

Genghis Khat happily ate each piece from the palm of

her hand and when he was done licking it clean, would nudge her hand for more.

And so it went.

Maggie ate the next three-fourths of her sandwich, one by one, and hand-fed Genghis Khat the rest of the turkey.

She'd carefully divided the pieces of turkey into four equal sections so that they were both finished with their lunch at approximately the same time.

Genghis Khat never tried to steal a single piece of turkey from her plate. He simply waited for her to feed him one piece at a time.

"You're the best cat ever, Genghis Khat," Maggie whispered to him. "So polite, so smart, so sweet." She scratched him on the head and fed him the final bit of turkey. "Last bite, darling."

Movement from across the table caught Maggie's attention and she realized Annie was still sitting in the booth with her. "Oh. You're still here?"

Annie smiled. "Still here. Your cat is beautiful. And I love the name."

Maggie completely agreed. Genghis Khat *was* beautiful. He was a scarred warrior with a beautiful soul. "I know."

"So who have you met in town so far?"

There it was.

The question.

Maggie considered questions to be a way for extroverts to manipulate and force introverts into participating in conversations they normally wouldn't.

Most of the time, Maggie simply refused to answer people's questions.

Either by giving non-answers or by not responding at all.

Of course, she knew most people considered that to be very rude, but honestly, Maggie just didn't care.

This time, in response to Annie's question, Maggie gave a half-hearted shrug in response, which to her meant she was making a real effort.

She wasn't sure how she'd been roped into eating at the diner, but now she was trapped in this booth with a ton of people between her and the door, and it hadn't escaped her notice that no one seemed inclined to leave anytime soon.

However, Annie *had* brought her this incredibly delicious meal that *almost* made up for Maggie having to interact with people.

"Well, let's take care of that right now," Annie said.

Maggie had no idea what that meant, but she was pretty sure she wasn't going to like it.

That turned out to be the understatement of the century.

Six

GENGHIS KHAT HEARTILY approved of this diner-place where Bygul had transported him earlier that day.

He'd had no idea when he walked in that he'd be treated to so many tasty, meaty morsels in such a short amount of time.

First, he'd wandered the diner, enjoying snack after snack.

Then, when Maggie had come to pick him up, she'd stayed and fed him more tasty, meaty morsels.

This was definitely his second favorite place on earth, the first being the recliner at their house, where he loved to stretch out on Maggie's lap.

He was so busy enjoying the taste-testing that he completely forgot he was supposed to be helping Maggie interact with the people at the diner.

Luckily, Annie, the woman who had brought him the cream in a saucer and the meaty morsels on a plate, took care of that task for him.

When they were done eating, Annie stood, grabbed Maggie by the arm and started dragging her from table to table, introducing her to everyone in the diner.

Genghis Khat followed, feeling a little put out that Annie wasn't bothering to introduce him as well.

Maggie took care of that, though, because she was the best human companion ever.

She scooped him up from the floor and proceeded to introduce him to everyone she met.

Annie would say, "This is Maggie. Maggie, these are the Donnelly sisters, Kate, Mary Lou and Hannah."

Then Maggie would nod and say, "This is Genghis Khat. He's the best cat in the world." Only Maggie never said the same thing about him twice. She came up with new ways to introduce him every time.

"This is Genghis Khat. He's a warrior with the scars to prove it."

"This is Genghis Khat. He has the most amazing purr. It rumbles like a steam engine."

"This is Genghis Khat. He's a hunter who specializes in decapitating his prey."

By the time they finished with all the introductions, Genghis Khat felt about ten feet tall. He hadn't realized all those wonderful things about himself.

Of course, he knew he was a good hunter, but he didn't know that about his purr or that Maggie loved his scars.

She really was the best human companion ever.

MAGGIE GOT THROUGH THE ORDEAL OF BEING introduced to so many people in such a short amount of time by focusing on Genghis Khat. She spent time in between introductions coming up with new ways to describe the best cat in the world.

Suddenly the terror of speaking with new people was almost fun. It was like a game.

A game of words and a way to let Genghis Khat know how much she appreciated him.

It got her through the endless rounds of conversations until finally she had met every single person in the diner for lunch that day.

Grateful she'd survived the onslaught, Maggie was edging toward the door when Annie exclaimed, "You have to come to the party Saturday night."

Gasps of shock resounded through the room, making it pretty obvious that no one else agreed with Annie's declaration.

"Oh, I'm not much for parties," Maggie said with a shake of her head.

She couldn't help but notice how relieved everyone appeared.

"Oh, but you haven't met everyone yet. Until you meet everyone, we won't know if—" Annie broke off with a look of consternation on her face.

Maggie was probably supposed to ask a question at that point, something like "What won't you know?" But she figured this was just another tactic to get her to engage in the conversation, and would probably result in her being manipulated into attending this party.

As Maggie considered the word party to be synonymous with hell on earth, she had no intention of being manipulated in such an obvious way.

So she simply stood there and waited.

When Annie never finished her sentence, Maggie decided it was time to move on. "I have to go now," she said.

Annie had never given her the check, so Maggie wasn't sure how much her meal had cost, but she set a couple twenties onto the counter on her way out.

THE MINUTE THE DOOR CLOSED BEHIND MAGGIE, Annie whirled around and glared at the shifters in the diner. "You should all be ashamed of yourselves. Just because she's human doesn't mean we can't be nice."

"You invited a human to a shifter party, Annie. What were you thinking?" Paul demanded.

"I was thinking that most of our eligible men and women aren't even here in the diner today. She could be the mate of any one of them. I figured most of them will be at the party Saturday night, which makes it the perfect gathering for her to find her mate."

"There's no way that human is the mate of any shifter," Bob Wilson said.

"How can you say that, Bob?" Annie demanded. "Her mother's a shifter, for heaven's sake!"

"Yeah, a shifter who couldn't wait to get away from her shifter roots. You never met Sarah Madison, but let me tell you, she was something else," Bob said. "The woman did everything she could to kill the cougar inside her and then she left this town and deliberately mated with a human. She did nothing to pull him into our world and instead, immersed herself into his. Worse, she had not a shred of compassion, honor or loyalty, and as far as I can tell, her daughter's nothing but a miniature Sarah."

"You don't even know her," Annie said.

"I know she was pretty damn unfriendly when she came to my office last month," Bob said. "And I know that nothing I saw in her today convinced me she wasn't anything but a clone of her angry, hateful mother."

"Don't be ridiculous. Someone who's full of anger and hate can't hide that from us, you know that. Emotions have a scent, Bob, and the only thing I scented around Maggie today was anxiety and uncertainty. It seems to me the only one lacking compassion around here is you." She sent a glare around the room. "All of you."

JACKSON WAS SITTING IN HIS OFFICE THE NEXT day, just about to bite into the burger he'd picked up from the diner on his lunch break when Connie appeared in the doorway, a giant grin on her face.

Jackson sighed and set down his burger.

This was not going to be good.

Anything that made Connie smile that widely was sure to be a disaster for him and hilarious for everyone else.

"What is it, Connie?"

"The crazy cat lady's on line one again."

"You're joking."

"Nope."

"What's the problem now? Cat climb a tree?"

"Oh no. Apparently the catnappers are back." Connie barely got the words out before she burst into laughter.

"You've got to be kidding me."

"Nope. She's quite serious. She wants you to send Danny back out, only this time he has to actually do his job and dust for fingerprints and take a cast of the shoe print in her flower bed."

Jackson dropped his head into his hands, then without

even looking, grabbed his headset, hit the button for line one and answered the call.

Five minutes later, he was convinced that Maggie Winters was nuttier than a Planters factory.

She was absolutely convinced someone kept breaking into her house to steal her cat.

"Lady, why would anyone want your cat?"

"A better question would be why *wouldn't* they want him? I'll have you know that Genghis Khat is both a warrior and a lover. He's utterly perfect in every way and there's no other cat like him. Anyone would be thrilled to have him as a companion cat, and I daresay, many of those people wouldn't hesitate to catnap him if necessary. Now why don't you do your job and catch the crooks who keep traumatizing the two of us?"

"Have you tried the diner yet?"

"Why on earth would he be at the diner? Genghis Khat may have escaped the catnapper yesterday and found refuge in the diner, but there's no guarantee he'll manage to do that again. He needs rescuing!"

Jackson heaved a huge sigh, then said, "I'm going to put you on hold for a moment, ma'am. I'll be right back." He didn't wait for a reply, just stabbed the hold button and yelled, "Connie, call the diner. See if the cat's shown up over there."

A few minutes later, Connie appeared in his office door, once more grinning like a loon. "You're psychic, Sheriff. The cat walked into the diner ten seconds into my conversation with Bud."

"Wonderful. I hope this isn't going to become a daily occurrence."

Connie chuckled. "Well, if it is, you might want to start eating your lunch at the diner rather than bringing it back here. Maybe then you'll catch those catnappers in the act."

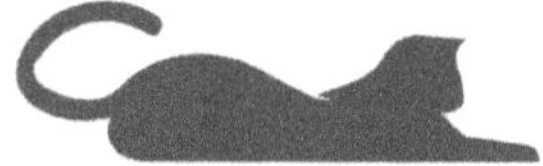

"WHAT DO YOU MEAN MY CAT'S AT THE DINER again? What is up with these catnappers?"

"Well, ma'am, I think you should perhaps consider the possibility that your cat is managing to escape your house on his own."

"Seriously? Sheriff, I don't have a whole lot of confidence in your investigative skills if *that's* the conclusion you've come to. Do you have any idea how far of a walk it is from my house to the diner? It takes me a good fifteen minutes by car. Are you seriously suggesting my cat walked that distance all by himself, all without being attacked by any of the local wildlife?"

The sheriff sighed. "All I'm saying, ma'am, is we don't have the resources to investigate missing cats. Maybe get a better lock for your windows. Have a good day, ma'am."

Then, quite unbelievably, *he hung up on her.*

"Oh, that man. He makes me crazy!" Maggie grabbed her purse and stormed out to her car.

The entire way to the diner, she fumed and mimicked his superior attitude, sneering, "I'm sorry, *ma'am*, your cat just isn't important enough for us to investigate his disappearance. *Bastard.*"

By the time she got to the diner, she was so angry, she completely forgot to be nervous. She stormed inside and immediately started searching under every table.

She didn't even pause to greet any of the people whose tables she was peeking beneath, regardless of whether she'd met them the day before or not.

"Hey, Maggie!" Annie called from behind the counter. "Genghis Khat's around here somewhere."

Maggie waved a hand in acknowledgment and kept peeking under tables, refusing to make eye contact or greet anyone along the way.

She was peripherally aware of the conversations above her pausing every time she peeked under a table, then starting up again as she moved on.

A few people tried to engage her in conversation, greeting her by name, but she just focused on the job at hand and ignored their overtures.

Finally, at the table in the opposite corner from the diner's door, she found Genghis Khat sprawled on top of a pair of boots.

Maggie didn't acknowledge the owner of those boots in any way.

She simply crawled under the table, scooped up Genghis Khat and backed out with him in her arms.

She ignored the sound of the owner of those boots chuckling and refused to look at him when he reached out to pat Genghis Khat on the head.

She climbed to her feet and turned away from the table, intending to leave immediately, but found Annie blocking her way.

"I've got you and Genghis Khat all set up in the same booth as last time, Maggie," Annie said, nodding to the booth across the way.

A saucer of milk was already sitting on the table.

"So what are you thinking today, Maggie? Turkey club again, or maybe a tuna melt, or the meatloaf or—"

Maggie sighed. "Let's try a tuna melt this time."

Genghis Khat let out a loud, rumbling purr and Maggie grinned, barely registering Annie's, "You got it," as she walked away.

"Yes, I know," Maggie murmured to Genghis Khat as she headed for the booth. "Tuna makes you *very* happy."

She'd barely settled in the booth, Genghis Khat still in her arms, when two women swooped into the seat across from her. Between the two of them, they were carrying three wine glasses and two unopened bottles of wine, both of them red.

"Hi. I'm Kate and this is Olivia, in case you don't remember us."

Maggie did.

"Call me Livi. And we love your cat."

Maggie smiled a bit. "Did you hear that, Genghis Khat? They like you." She settled him on the seat beside her, then watched as he immediately set both front paws on the table in front of him and stared across it at Kate and Livi.

"Sorry, no wine for you, Mr. Khat," Livi said as she opened one of the bottles of wine. "But the good news is that means more for us." She poured them each a glass and lifted hers in the air. "Cheers."

Kate held hers up, so Maggie did the same and watched as they tapped their glasses to hers.

This was an odd ritual she'd never before participated in.

Both the toasting and the drinking.

"Bottoms up," Livi said and she drained her glass.

Kate followed suit.

Maggie wasn't sure this was a good idea, especially since she had to drive herself and Genghis Khat back home later, but she *was* curious to know what red wine tasted like, so she tried a sip, found it to be palatable and took a larger drink.

Surprisingly, she didn't hate it.

She'd had a sip of champagne once and the bubbles had made her shudder.

This was smooth though and rather tasty.

She had another gulp and then drained the glass as she'd seen the other two women do.

"Right on!" Livi exclaimed, then poured them each another round.

This glass, they drank slowly.

Maggie savored the taste and found it surprisingly soothing.

She might have to add a red wine subscription to her monthly orders.

"So, how are you liking Greensboro so far?" Kate asked. "Is it super different from the last place you lived? Did you live in a big city or a small town like ours?"

Questions.

Always questions.

Maggie shrugged and took another large gulp of wine.

"Don't mind Kate," Livi said. "She chatters like that all the time. You don't have to answer her questions, especially since she rarely gives anyone a chance to get a word in edgewise."

"Hey!"

"You know it's true, Kate." Livi topped off Maggie's glass.

"That's beside the point," Kate said.

Maggie took another big gulp.

So good.

Genghis Khat lost interest in staring at the women and dropped his front feet back down into the booth, where he circled and kneaded the seat for a couple minutes before finally curling up and falling asleep.

Maggie found him to be so adorable lying there, she turned her attention to petting him, and for long moments, lost track of the conversation as Livi and Kate argued good-naturedly.

She drank down her glass of red with her left hand while adoring Genghis Khat with her right.

"So, Maggie." Kate dragged her attention back to the two of them. "Do you have a boyfriend? Girlfriend? Gender neutral friend? Lover? Significant other? Whatever you want to call them?"

"Uh." Maggie snickered, unexpectedly amused by Kate's frenetic questioning style. "No."

"Cool. Would you like one? And if so, which would you choose? Boyfriend? Girlfriend? Gender neutral—"

"Please, do *not* go through that list again," Livi said as she filled Maggie's glass once more.

"Psh." Kate waved a hand. "So?"

For some reason, Maggie was charmed enough that for once, she didn't mind answering a question. "I guess boyfriend if I wanted one, but I don't."

"Well, why not?"

Maggie shrugged and drained her glass. This was not a conversation she'd ever expected to have, but definitely not with two virtual strangers.

Livi filled Maggie's glass again, which was a really welcome development, given the subject matter.

Maggie took a gulp.

"Come on, why not?" Kate asked.

"Why not what?" Maggie couldn't remember the question. What were they talking about again?

"Why don't you want a boyfriend?"

"It's not that I don't want one. It's that people don't like me and it's just better to not even try. A boyfriend would be too much hard work—trying to make him like me, trying to be whoever he wanted me to be instead of who I am. No. I'm better off alone."

At that moment, Genghis Khat stood and put his front paws on Maggie's left shoulder and nuzzled her cheek, thus reminding her that she was not alone at all.

"Aw, you're the best, Genghis Khat." She scooped him up and kissed his forehead, right above his nose. "I love you, baby boy."

Annie arrived at that moment, delivering Maggie's tuna melt, Livi's burger and fries and Kate's fish and chips. "Enjoy, ladies."

The rest of the afternoon passed in a bit of a blur for Maggie.

When they finished eating, Livi, Kate and Annie, who ended her shift early to join them, dragged Maggie to the local salon, where they got manicures and pedicures.

Unbelievably, they insisted that Genghis Khat accompany them and no one at the salon protested his presence. Instead, all the workers in the salon fussed over the cat and treated him like the king he was.

The women talked and laughed while their nails were being painted, and enjoyed a third bottle of wine provided by the salon.

Maggie chose a brilliant red for her nails and spent a bit of time envisioning all the different outfits in her closet that would look amazing against that red.

Once their nails were done, the women dragged Maggie and Genghis Khat to the only movie theater in town where they watched a terrifying film about a serial killer clown.

The women ate too much popcorn and washed it down with a gallon of coke, all the while cringing and squealing and peeking between their fingers at the screen during the intensely scary parts.

Genghis Khat was the only one who seemed undisturbed by the events onscreen. He snoozed quite happily in Maggie's lap the entire movie, not even waking when Maggie shrieked and sent popcorn sailing everywhere.

The movie was freaky and terrifying and Maggie wouldn't give up the experience for anything in the world.

In the end, it was the most beautiful day of Maggie's life.

By the time they made it back to the diner, Maggie was no longer feeling the effects of the wine, but she was giddy with the realization that at thirty-six years of age, she may have finally made her very first, real friends.

Seven

WHEN BYGUL SHOWED up and cast a bit of magic at the kitchen window the next day, Genghis Khat was ready for him.

He sailed through the window and just like that, Bygul transported them both to the alley behind the diner.

Genghis Khat decided he was beginning to like this job. The diner was a wondrous place, full of yummy food (the tuna the day before had been divine) and people willing to scratch any itch he had.

"Come along, G.K." Bygul said and led the way around to the front of the diner, where they stood at the big picture window and peered inside. "Are there any new people inside or have we been wasting our time with the same people over and over again?"

How in the world was Genghis Khat supposed to know the answer to that question? He didn't pay attention to people's faces. He mostly saw their shoes and their boots and sometimes their fingers that came down to offer a tasty morsel or a head scratch.

And he needed to be inside the diner if he wanted to identify them by scent.

"Right. Let's go inside then," Bygul said. "I've got a bit more time this morning, so I'm going to stick around, just to see what's going on in here. We might need to choose a new place tomorrow if the diner's a bust."

A new place! What if there wasn't any food or head-scratching humans at the new place?

MAGGIE WASN'T HAPPY WHEN SHE DISCOVERED FOR the third day in a row that Genghis Khat had somehow disappeared from her house.

This time, the window over the kitchen sink was open.

Maggie had tried to open the window when she'd first moved in, but it had been stuck and she'd been unable to budge it.

Yet somehow, while she'd been cleaning upstairs, someone had managed to pry the window open and entice Genghis Khat outside.

She had no idea how this kept happening, especially since paranoia had her checking all the doors and windows before going to bed at night and once again when waking each morning.

She'd even closed her bedroom door the last two nights to keep Genghis Khat close, which had seemed a genius plan yesterday morning when she woke to a paw on the cheek and kitty breath.

Her mistake had been thinking the danger was over when he hadn't been stolen in the middle of the night. She'd gone out into the garden as usual yesterday and when she'd returned, the window in the study had been open again and Genghis Khat nowhere to be seen.

Today, she'd been determined there wouldn't be a third catnapping.

More paranoid than ever, she'd kept Genghis Khat with her as she moved about the house, dusting and vacuuming.

Unfortunately, Genghis Khat hated the vacuum cleaner and he'd gotten away from her when she'd opened the guest bedroom door. She'd raced after him, but somehow it was already too late.

The window was open and Genghis Khat and his catnapper were long gone.

She couldn't understand it. She'd been seconds behind him and yet somehow, he'd managed to leave the house and completely disappear.

Not a single car or person was in sight of the house in any direction and yet there was no denying the cat was missing.

This time, Maggie didn't even bother to call the sheriff's

office. The man was infuriating and if he wasn't willing to do his job and investigate these catnappings, Maggie would damn well do it for him.

At this point, she was fairly certain the catnapper was just messing with her. He probably had some secret way of getting into her house and back out again without being seen.

So Maggie's first step—after rescuing Genghis Khat again, of course—would be to find the catnapper's secret entrance.

And block it forever.

Grabbing her car keys, Maggie stormed out of the house and for the third time in as many days, drove into town, headed for the diner.

She was annoyed, yes, and worried about Genghis Khat, of course, but there was a tiny part of her that was happy to have an excuse to go into town again because maybe Annie would be working this morning or maybe Livi and Kate would be there having lunch.

Maybe even all three of them would be there and she'd get to hang out with her friends again.

JACKSON HAD TO ADMIT IT WAS PURE CURIOSITY that had him sitting in a booth toward the back of the diner the following day, rather than ordering his lunch to-go.

"Well, Sheriff, it sure is nice to see you here in the middle of the day," Annie said with a grin. "You here to meet our resident cat or the human?"

"Definitely the cat," Jackson said dryly.

At that moment, a huge gray monstrosity leapt onto the bench seat across from Jackson.

"Good lord, is that the cat in question?"

"The very one," Annie said cheerfully as the cat glared balefully at Jackson over the top of the table.

"He doesn't seem too happy to see me," Jackson observed.

"Well, you are sitting in his booth."

Jackson gave Annie an incredulous look. "You gave the cat his own booth?"

"Not exactly, but Maggie sat here the first day she came to collect Genghis Khat and it's kind of been her booth ever since."

"Ever since two days ago," Jackson said dryly.

"Well, no one's really wanted to use it since, so..."

Jackson wasn't even surprised to hear this.

Shifters could be utterly ridiculous sometimes.

He leaned forward a bit and called to the other diners, "What, did you think her humanity's catching or something?"

"Or something," David Humphreys growled.

Jackson shook his head.

Wolves.

So damn superstitious.

Jackson sat back in the booth and stared at the cat across from him.

Genghis Khat—a name so ridiculous, Jackson couldn't help but smile at the audacity of it—was sitting straight and tall and staring right at him.

Over the next several minutes, Jackson indulged in a staring contest with a domesticated cat.

It was ridiculous, but once he'd started, he couldn't figure out how to extricate himself without appearing weak to the other shifters, not to mention the damn cat.

"There you are, Genghis Khat!"

The staring contest was mercifully ended when the cat was suddenly swept up into a woman's arms.

And what a woman!

Jackson was struck dumb at the sight of her.

She was wearing a bright green dress that came to mid-thigh and the sassiest sandals he'd ever seen. They had ribbons that wrapped around and around her calves, accentuating what had to be the sexiest legs he'd seen in a long time.

Her hair fell in long, brown waves almost to her waist and her bangs fell across her eyes like curtains.

She peeked at him, just once, giving him a glimpse of hazel eyes, before she plopped into the seat across from him, cuddling the ridiculous cat in her arms.

Her scent reached him in a delicate, floral wave that had the panther inside stretching and pressing against his skin.

Before Jackson could really do anything other than blink

at this vision in front of him, Annie showed up with two plates. She slid the one with a burger in front of Jackson and the other—a tuna melt, it looked like—in front of the human.

"Hi, Maggie," Annie exclaimed. "I hope you don't mind. I went ahead and put in an order for a tuna melt for you. I noticed how much Genghis Khat enjoyed the tuna yesterday and since the sheriff is here for his lunch, I thought it'd be nice if the two of you could keep each other company."

Jackson couldn't help but notice that Maggie never took her attention from the cat in her lap the entire time Annie was speaking. However, the minute Annie said sheriff, Maggie's head came flying up and her eyes jerked from Annie to Jackson.

"You!" she exclaimed.

Jackson opened his mouth, without any real inkling as to what he was going to say, but whatever it was, he didn't have a chance to say it, because Maggie cut him off in a rush of words.

"I don't appreciate you dismissing my concerns. There's quite obviously a catnapper at work in this community causing all kinds of mischief. Maybe it's just some prankster, but I'm not finding it funny. And it's your job to stop criminal activity."

She stood and swept from the booth. She had the cat cradled in her left arm and used her right to grab the plate with the tuna melt on it. "You should be ashamed of yourself. Your deputy refused to take fingerprints the first time Genghis Khat went missing, and here we are, two days later with three unsolved catnappings you haven't even bothered to begin to investigate. Well, I'll tell you what, if you won't solve this spree of catnappings, I will!" With that, she turned on her heel and flounced out of the diner.

Silence fell in her wake until the diner's door opened again and Maggie poked her head back in to call, "I'll bring the plate back tomorrow, Annie, if that's okay."

"Sure, sure!"

"Just charge it to my account, or better yet, charge it to your condescending, inept sheriff's account!" With that, she was gone again.

"Ooooh, doggie," Travis Norton exclaimed. "You done riled up the human, Jackson."

Jackson didn't reply. He was too busy processing what had just happened.

"Jackson, honey, you okay?" Annie was starting to look concerned.

She couldn't possibly be as concerned as Jackson was though.

"What's the matter, Sheriff?" David's wife, Natalie asked. "Haven't you ever seen a human before?"

"Sure I have, Natalie. Just haven't met one that's my mate before." With that, he lunged from the booth and raced toward the door, with only one thing in mind.

Soothing his mate's temper.

"Darn that sheriff, Genghis Khat." Maggie sat in her car in the diner's parking lot, fuming. "He ruined everything. I was looking forward to chatting with Annie again. Although there *were* a lot of people in the diner I hadn't met yet, so maybe it was better to just get out of there. No use pushing my luck."

Genghis Khat, who was sitting on the console between the two front seats, rubbed his head against her shoulder and let out a deep, rumbling purr.

"I know, baby." Maggie lifted a hand and stroked it all the way down his back. "You're the best kitty ever."

A knock on the window startled both of them, making Maggie jump and Genghis Khat hiss fiercely.

A peek at the side window told Maggie it was the idiot sheriff knocking.

Damn.

"It's okay, Genghis Khat. Everything's going to be just fine." Maggie stroked him several times, soothing down his fur and crooning to him.

Interestingly, the sheriff didn't knock again, just stood outside the door waiting patiently.

Or maybe not so patiently, Maggie didn't know.

Still, he didn't knock or hurry her along, so Maggie counted that as a tiny point in his favor.

One tiny point that barely made a dent in all the ones he'd racked up as marks against him.

Finally, she turned and rolled the window down a couple inches. She stared at him, but didn't say anything. After all, she wasn't the one knocking on his car door window. She had nothing to say.

He was silent for a minute before he finally seemed to realize she was waiting on him to speak. "Would you mind stepping out of the car for a minute?"

Maggie scowled. What could he possibly want from her now? She turned to Genghis Khat and said, "Be good, boy. I'll be right back."

She opened the door and the sheriff stepped forward to offer a hand.

She froze and stared at his hand.

What was he doing?

He just waited.

Was she supposed to give him something?

Well, he *was* a cop. Maybe he wanted her license and registration.

Or maybe he paid for her lunch and wanted her to pay him back.

She couldn't imagine what else he'd want her to give him.

She felt Genghis Khat's paws on her shoulders and glanced back to see that he was now standing on his hind legs and peering over her shoulder at the sheriff.

She turned back to the sheriff just in time to see him reach toward her.

She shrank back, but all he did was catch both of her hands in his and gently pull her from the car.

Oh.

He'd been offering his hand to help.

Now Maggie felt foolish.

At least she hadn't tried to give him money or her license or anything like that.

Genghis Khat meowed at her and she turned to see he was now sitting in the drivers' seat, watching her and the sheriff.

"It's okay, Genghis Khat. We won't be long."

The sheriff closed the door and pulled her toward him.

That was when Maggie realized he still had hold of both her hands.

He guided her around so her back was to the car, then stepped in so he was standing right in front of her.

Closer than she was usually comfortable with.

He was in her space and Maggie was usually very territorial about her space.

This was her space, that was his space, and never the twain shall meet.

Except right then, her space and his space were all tangled up together and she was feeling a bit lightheaded.

"Breathe, Maggie."

She dragged in a deep breath. "You know my name."

"You called my office the past two days, gave your name each time."

Maggie scowled at the reminder. "Yes, and you didn't take my concerns seriously."

He raised an eyebrow. "I took your concerns seriously enough to send a deputy out to your house."

Well, she supposed that was true. It wasn't his fault his deputy had refused to dust for fingerprints.

"I also tracked your cat to the diner and you got him back both days, didn't you?"

Maggie sighed. Well, when he put it like that, sure. "Yes, but you haven't done anything to keep this from happening again. Today was the third time someone opened a window at my house and stole my cat."

"Right."

From the look on the sheriff's face, Maggie was pretty sure he didn't agree with her assessment of the situation. Still, he didn't argue with her, which was probably another point in his favor.

"Well, how about I come out right now and help you problem-solve? We can take a look around, see where the intruder might be getting in or possibly how—" he hesitated, then continued, "—Genghis Khat might be getting out."

She wasn't sure what that hesitation meant, but had a feeling it was related to her cat in some way. The sheriff probably thought she hadn't noticed, but he'd been in a pretty intense stare-down with Genghis Khat when she'd arrived at the diner.

She'd planned to admonish him for trying to intimidate her cat, but then she'd found out he was the sheriff and she had a much bigger lecture to deliver.

Oh, well, she'd just save that one for next time.

"Maggie?"

"Fine, Sheriff. You can follow me back to the house."

"First, call me Jackson."

Maggie hesitated, then said softly, "Jackson."

He smiled at her, then stepped back, pulling her with him. He opened the car door and held it as she climbed in. "I'll meet you at your house. Drive safe." He closed the car door and stood there, hands on hips, watching as she pulled out of the parking lot and headed toward home.

Within minutes, he was behind her on the winding roads leading out of town.

By the time they reached the house, Maggie was a bundle of nerves.

Genghis Khat could obviously sense her nerves because he'd paced in the passenger side seat the entire trip home.

Scooping Genghis Khat into her arms, Maggie met Jackson on the front porch, and let him into the house, feeling more nervous than ever.

She'd never had a man over to her place before—any place, not just this one.

"So I thought I should look for a secret entrance," she

said. "I figure that's the only way someone could sneak into my house without me knowing it."

"What about the locks? If your Aunt Becky gave keys to anyone—"

"I changed the locks when I moved in. No one has the keys but me."

"Right, then. Let's get to the searching."

As strange as it was, the afternoon and evening went by quickly.

Maggie found Jackson's presence to be both soothing and agitating, all at the same time.

Genghis Khat followed them from room to room as they searched for a false entrance. They tapped all the walls, explored every closet in depth, and found nothing.

Jackson spent some time looking at both the study window and the kitchen window and couldn't find anything wrong with either lock.

"This just isn't possible, Genghis Khat," Maggie said, hands on hips.

Genghis Khat was sitting in the center of the kitchen table, watching carefully as Jackson flipped the lock on the window back and forth.

"I just don't understand how you keep getting out. I know you're not doing it on your own, but I don't know how someone's getting in."

"Well, you could certainly have a security system added, wire the windows so the alarm blares when they're opened, but it seems like overkill."

Maggie sighed. "Yeah. I guess. Well, thanks for trying to help, Sheriff."

He raised an eyebrow.

"Jackson."

He smiled. "It was my pleasure, Maggie. It's getting on to dinner time. I was going to go to the diner, if you'd like to join me."

Maggie shook her head. "Oh, no." She'd spent more than enough time socializing and talking for one day, and while the sheriff wasn't quite the idiot she'd once thought him, she needed him to leave now.

She'd enjoyed listening to him speak and watching him wander through her house. She'd enjoyed watching his capable hands knocking on walls and testing the locks on her doors and windows.

She'd enjoyed the feel of his hand in hers when he'd led her down the stairs and into the kitchen just a few moments before.

But it was too much.

Entirely too much for one day.

"Time to go, Sheriff." Maggie hurried toward the front door and flung it open.

He followed at a more leisurely pace, then stopped right next to her and slid one broad hand around to the back of her neck, where he cradled her head.

He nudged her chin up with his other hand and leaned down and kissed her.

It wasn't her first kiss.

There were a few teenaged fumblings in her past.

And one tentative kiss with a roommate she'd had a girl-crush on in her early twenties.

This, though, was her first kiss from a man.

And oh, what a man.

His kiss was gentle and light and sent shivers down her back.

He came back for more and laid a series of kisses on her lips, one after the other, making her shiver in delight.

Her hands came up of their own accord and latched onto his shirt where they clung as he coaxed her lips open and swept his tongue inside for a hotter, more devastating kiss than she'd ever known.

Long moments later, he pulled back, then leaned down and kissed her again, one short kiss that left her breathless.

"Lock the door behind me, Maggie," he murmured against her lips.

She nodded dazedly and followed him out the door.

He stopped on the porch and gently nudged her back inside the house. "I'll see you tomorrow. Close the door and lock it now."

She nodded again.

He stepped back and in a daze, she closed the door and locked it. She stood there and listened as he said, "Sweet dreams, Maggie mine." She staggered to the picture window and watched as he sauntered down her front walkway, climbed into his car and drove off into the night.

Maggie sagged down onto the couch, touched shaky fingers to her lips and let out a soft whimper.

Genghis Khat leapt up onto her lap, nudged her chin and she caught him up in her arms, hugging him close in an almost compulsive move. "Oh, Genghis Khat," she whispered. "What just happened?"

Eight

GENGHIS KHAT DIDN'T understand humans at all.

He wasn't sure why his Maggie was shaking, but he knew it had something to do with that sheriff, so he spent the night guarding his human and making a plan to avoid the sheriff from now on.

Unfortunately, that plan was pretty much destroyed when Bygul showed up the next morning.

"We've found Maggie's mate," Bygul explained, "so instead of going to the diner today, we're going to the barbershop where her mate has an appointment."

Genghis Khat didn't like this idea at all. He doubted the barbershop would be a food paradise like the diner.

However, to get Maggie the mate she needed so they could stay in this town, Genghis Khat was willing to make the supreme sacrifice.

It was a good thing too because the next thing he knew, he was inside a long, narrow room that had all kinds of hair on the floor, but no tasty morsels.

Genghis Khat growled his displeasure at Bygul.

"Oh, get over it. There's Maggie's mate. Go make friends with him."

Genghis Khat was horrified when he realized Bygul was referring to the sheriff.

The sheriff who'd left his scent in every room of their house the day before and who'd upset Maggie so much that after he'd left, she'd been a mess, constantly asking Genghis Khat to explain what had just happened.

Apparently, the answer was that Maggie had met her mate.

And Genghis Khat *hated* him.

MAXWELL HAD JUST FINISHED SHAVING THE BACK of Jackson's neck when Maggie's crazy cat appeared out of nowhere and leapt onto Jackson's lap.

Both Maxwell and Jackson let out yelps of surprise.

Laughter sounded around the room as the cat from hell began kneading Jackson's legs, full claws extended.

Jackson winced and tried to lift the cat away, but it just sank its claws in deeper.

"Okay, okay. Ow, ow, ow, you freaky feline." In desperation, Jackson shoved his hands between the cat and his family jewels.

Just in case.

"Damn." With one hand blocking the cat from full access, Jackson extricated his phone with the other and called Connie. "Get ahold of Maggie and let her know her cat's at the barbershop today."

Five minutes later, Maggie burst into the shop. She must have already been in town to have gotten there so quickly.

She froze for one moment when she caught sight of Genghis Khat on Jackson's lap.

"Hey, sweetheart," Jackson said, sending her his best smile.

Maggie's face darkened in response. "Is *this* why you refused to investigate the catnappings?"

"Huh?"

"And then insisted on coming over last night to *help*?" She made quotes in the air around help. "Were you really helping at all or were you just setting things up for the next catnapping?"

"What? Maggie, no!"

"Well, what else am I supposed to think, Jackson? Someone keeps stealing my cat and here you are, cuddling him like he's *your* cat, not mine!"

"Does this *look* like cuddling? Because I assure you there is no cuddling happening over here." Jackson winced as the demon cat flexed its claws.

Maggie made a sound of frustration, stormed toward him and swept Genghis Khat into her arms.

Jackson winced as ten claws peeled from his skin all at once.

Maggie whirled and stalked toward the door.

The cat stared over her shoulder at Jackson with what he would swear was a smug look on its face.

"Maggie, wait!" Jackson jumped up, peeled a couple bills from his wallet, pressed them into Maxwell's hand and hurried after her, a symphony of "Good luck!" and "You're going to need it!" following him out the door.

MAGGIE STAMPED TOWARD HER CAR, FUMING.

She couldn't believe Jackson was trying to steal her cat!

"Maggie, hold up!" Jackson darted into her path and held out his hands in the universal stop position.

She skidded to a halt and scowled at him.

"Sweetheart, I *promise* I am not the one stealing your cat. No one was more surprised than me when he jumped into my lap at the barbershop."

Maggie eyed him suspiciously. He sounded sincere, but she just wasn't sure whether to believe him or not.

"I assume you didn't touch your windows or doors after I left last night."

"Of course not. That didn't seem to matter today though."

"What do you mean?"

"Genghis Khat was with me all morning long. He was sitting right on the kitchen table and we were having a lovely conversation." She paused at the odd look on Jackson's face, but before she could interpret what it meant, he smiled and the look was gone.

"Go on. You were talking with the cat and then what?"

"I turned away to get something out of a cabinet and when I turned back, he was gone. I searched everywhere, but he was nowhere to be found and all the windows and doors were closed tight. Now how do you explain that, Jackson?"

He looked perplexed. "Frankly, it's starting to sound a bit like god magic."

Maggie took a step back. "I don't believe in god or heaven or hell or any of that." She saw no condemnation on his face, which she had to admit, was a huge relief. "There's just no scientific proof that any of it really exists."

Jackson grinned. "Valid point, but I'm not *really* talking about that kind of god. I'm more talking about *the* gods, as in plural. You know, the ones who occasionally like to meddle in—" he cleared his throat "—people's affairs. This sounds like the work of a mischievous god."

Maggie thought his theory was as lacking in scientific evidence as every other god theory she'd ever heard, but since at this point, she had zero *logical* explanations, she supposed she might have to accept an illogical one instead. And now that she thought about it, an illogical explanation might be the only one that actually made sense, in some weird, alternate universe kind of way, of course.

She hefted Genghis Khat away from her shoulder and held him up high so she could see his face. "So, what's the story, Genghis Khat? Are the gods responsible for you coming into town every day?"

Genghis Khat let out a sound that seemed to start as a purr and ended as a meow. This was unexpected as he rarely responded to any of her questions.

"Well, I wouldn't say that's a no." She settled him back against her chest, so that he was once again resting his head on her shoulder, and smiled at Jackson. "Of course, I'm not sure it was a yes, either, so I guess that means it's not outside the realm of possibility. A weird and crazy realm, to be sure, but I've been unable to come up with any other explanation."

"Crazy." Jackson grinned. "Right. Well, I have a couple other crazy things you should probably know. Why don't we head over to the diner? We can get some lunch and chat for a bit."

Maggie hesitated. Was she really up for yet another round of social interactions?

"I bet Genghis Khat would enjoy a treat and he must be getting a bit heavy to carry."

She supposed one more round wouldn't be so bad. Especially since most of the people in this town gave her a wide berth and didn't seem to take offense when she chose not to reply to their greetings. She started walking toward the diner, which was just a few doors down, and Jackson fell into step at her side.

When they reached the door of the diner, he opened it for her and rested a hand on her lower back to gently guide her into the restaurant.

She moved forward, intensely aware of the placement of his hand.

Genghis Khat shifted on her shoulder and hissed.

Jackson let out a yelp and jerked his hand away from her waist.

By this time, they were several steps into the restaurant and laughter swept like a wave through the diners.

"Having a bit of trouble there, are ya, Sheriff?" one of the diners called out.

Jackson let out a soft growl of annoyance.

Maggie glanced over the opposite shoulder from where Genghis Khat was.

Jackson had his hand to his mouth and was —licking it?

He saw her watching and jerked his hand back down, quickly covering it with his other one, but it was too late.

She'd already seen the scratch.

"Oh, Genghis Khat." She shook her head and made her way through the tables, ignoring the many greetings called her way, focused on reaching the booth she was starting to think of as belonging to her and Genghis Khat.

When she reached their table, she set him on it and bent

down to stare into his eyes. "Be nice to the sheriff and he might buy you a treat."

Jackson made a scoffing sound as he settled into the booth.

Maggie scowled, settled onto the bench across from him and said, "You'll never win him over with that attitude."

"Who says I *want* to win him over?"

Before Maggie could reply, Annie showed up to take their orders, which was really excellent timing. "Annie, what would you say if I told you that Jackson doesn't want to make friends with Genghis Khat?"

"I'd say he might as well give up on making friends with *you,* in that case."

Maggie grinned. "You already know me so well. I'll have the burger and fries today."

"Good choice. Anything for Genghis Khat?"

"I think just water to drink."

Genghis Khat let out a tiny growl, startling Maggie and making Annie laugh.

"Sounds like he doesn't agree with that choice," Annie observed.

"Okay, fine. A *small* saucer of milk." Maggie had been reading up on cat care and it turned out dairy wasn't the healthiest of choices for cats, but then again, Genghis Khat probably hadn't had much milk—or really any treats at all—in his life up to now, so maybe she should just let him enjoy his newfound good fortune.

"Jackson?" Annie asked.

Maggie stared across the table at Jackson and raised an eyebrow.

He let out a huff and said, "Bring the demon cat a can of tuna. And I'll have the burger and fries as well."

"You got it." Annie winked at Maggie and headed back to the kitchen.

"Interesting," Maggie said.

"What's that?"

"You not only believe in multiple gods, but also that my cat is possessed by a demon."

Jackson grinned. "Not exactly what I meant, but it'll do. Anyway, there's something I wanted to talk to you about."

"Yes?"

"You see, this town's a little—"

He seemed to be searching for the proper words, but Maggie already knew a bunch of them. "Unusual? Unique? Strange?"

He laughed. "Well, sure, all of the above, but that wasn't really what I was going to—"

"Maggie!" Kate shoved her way into Maggie's side of the booth. "I'm so excited! You and the sheriff are—"

"Kate!" Jackson snapped.

"—dating!" Kate glared across at Jackson who glared right back at her.

They weren't dating, were they? Based on Jackson's scowl, the answer was definitely not. Maggie ignored the sinking feeling inside and said, "Oh, um, no, of course—"

"We are," Jackson said. He reached across the table and grabbed Maggie's hand.

Maggie's eyes widened. She glanced from Jackson to Kate and back again. "We are?"

"We definitely are." He nodded emphatically.

"Oh, okay." She turned to Kate. "Yes?" She didn't really mean to say it like that, like it was a question, but she was still too stunned to really process what any of it meant. "Yes," she said again, this time with a bit more confidence.

Kate grinned, threw her arms around Maggie and hugged her tight.

Jackson still had hold of one of Maggie's hands and her other hand was busy petting Genghis Khat, who was stretched out on the table as if the entire thing belonged to him. So with neither hand being free, Maggie couldn't exactly hug Kate back, but that was okay because Maggie had zero experience with hugs and wasn't quite sure of the etiquette involved.

Before she could even decide whether she liked being on the receiving end of a hug, Kate pulled back and exclaimed, "You're perfect for each other!"

Jackson scowled.

He couldn't prove it, but he was pretty sure the damn cougar had done that on purpose.

The shifters in the diner weren't exactly making it a secret that they were all listening intently to Jackson's attempts to woo his mate.

If they thought he hadn't noticed how their conversations pretty much died the minute he said he wanted to talk to Maggie about something, they were crazy.

Then for Kate to show up right when he was about to blurt out the truth—her timing was entirely too suspicious. She had to have done it on purpose, he knew she had.

Then she'd actually demanded to know whether they were dating, not that Jackson believed that was the word she'd been about to use. She'd almost given away they were mates.

He glared at Kate as she gushed about them dating and how perfect they were for each other.

Jackson happened to agree, of course, but Kate needed to butt out so that he could prove it to Maggie, who clearly wasn't as certain as he was that they were meant to be together.

Maggie never really said anything in reply to Kate's babbling, but Jackson had already noticed that silence tended to be Maggie's go-to response when most people attempted to engage her in conversation.

He wasn't even convinced that she heard them half the time, but if she did, she was an expert at ignoring them.

In Kate's case, however, Maggie actually appeared to be listening to her if the tiny smirk on her face was any indication.

Finally, Kate's rambling dwindled away and she gave Maggie one last hug and exited the booth.

Jackson glared at Kate's back as she walked away, but then realized Maggie was watching and tried to school his face into a more neutral expression.

"Did you really mean that?" Maggie asked.

"Mean what?"

"That we're dating now."

Jackson grinned. "How could you possibly doubt it after last night's kiss?"

Maggie blushed, then shrugged one shoulder. "I just wasn't sure, that's all."

"Yes, well, the thing is, Maggie, um, I wanted to talk to you about the town because, you see—"

"Oh, you don't have to explain the town," Maggie said. "I already know it's a little weird. I mean, look at Genghis Khat." She spread her hands to indicate the ridiculous feline currently sprawled across the table.

Jackson couldn't believe the cat had exposed its belly to a roomful of predators.

Zero respect.

That's what the feline was showing him.

Jackson scowled down at the cat. Maybe if he pricked it with one of his claws.

Just a little bit.

He wouldn't actually hurt the cat, of course, just teach it a lesson.

"Jackson!"

He jumped, then looked up to find Maggie glaring at him.

Shit.

He surreptitiously curled his fingers a little. Thank goodness his claws were still retracted.

He cleared his throat. "Ah, sorry. What were you saying?"

"Just that it's a little weird for a restaurant to allow a cat inside, let alone a cat that sits on the tables. Aren't they worried about a visit from the health department?"

"Eh, not really. People in these parts—they're not that worried about a bit of fur in their food."

Someone snorted.

Jackson refused to look to see who it was.

Didn't matter anyway.

They were all bastards.

He should never have brought Maggie here. He should have suggested they go back to her house or that she come to his.

"Brother! Fancy meeting you here."

No. Freaking. Way.

Jackson glared as his twin brother, Jefferson, shoved his way into the booth, right next to Jackson's mate.

Jackson let out a small growl and fisted his hands.

He would *not* attack his brother in front of his mate.

He would *not*.

Later, however, all bets were off.

Jefferson grinned across the table at Jackson, as if he

knew exactly what Jackson was thinking, then turned to Maggie and grabbed the hand that was busy petting the demon cat. "You must be Maggie. I'm Jefferson, the handsome Hewitt."

Jackson rolled his eyes. Jefferson had been telling that ridiculous joke since they'd hit their teens and discovered girls.

Maggie giggled.

Jackson scowled.

That was the first time he'd heard her laugh and *Jefferson* was the one who made it happen.

Not cool.

It was now Jackson's mission in life to get Maggie to laugh.

Often.

And why was Maggie staring at Jefferson so intently? Damn his brother. He might just have to—

At that moment, Maggie turned and stared at Jackson with the same amount of concentration.

That's when Jackson realized what she was doing. She was obviously searching for differences, but he knew she'd never be able to tell them apart, as they really were identical in every way.

Maggie switched her attention back to Jefferson, studied him for a couple more beats, then shook her head and said, "Sorry, Jefferson, but I'm afraid Jackson has you beat in the handsome department."

Jackson burst into laughter.

Jefferson grinned. "I expect you have to say that, since you're–hmmm–*dating*. So *this* is the infamous Genghis Khat." He held out a hand for the demon cat to sniff and Jackson grinned in anticipation.

He would *not* be warning his ass of a brother that he was risking life and limb. Literally.

Genghis Khat rolled over and stretched to a standing position. He then nudged Jefferson's hand with his nose.

Jefferson chuckled and began petting the demon cat.

"Excuse me?" Jackson growled. "How is that right?"

Maggie giggled again, which admittedly, brightened Jackson's day, but he did *not* appreciate the smug look the cat sent him over its shoulder.

Damn cat!

Nine

THE LATEST HUMAN, who introduced himself as Handsome Hewitt, smelled a lot like the sheriff, only a bit wilder.

Genghis Khat liked that wildness.

He also liked that Handsome Hewitt made Maggie laugh.

Maybe Bygul had gotten it wrong.

Maybe the sheriff wasn't Maggie's mate after all. Maybe it was Handsome Hewitt instead.

It'd be an easy mistake to make since they smelled a lot alike.

Genghis Khat liked the idea that Handsome Hewitt was Maggie's mate and not the sheriff, so he decided to explore the situation further.

He climbed to his feet and nudged Handsome Hewitt's hand, just to see what he would do.

As it turned out, Handsome Hewitt took the nudge as an invitation to pet Genghis Khat. A nudge did mean that in certain situations. Maggie belonged to him, so of course a nudge to her hand meant pet me now.

A nudge to a stranger's hand, however, was often just a test.

To see what the stranger would do.

And to determine whether claws and teeth were required or not.

In this case, Genghis Khat decided they weren't required, mainly because the sheriff's scent had changed the minute Handsome Hewitt had joined them, going from a bit nervous and uncertain to irritated and impatient.

This led Genghis Khat to believe that the sheriff would be quite pleased if Genghis Khat clawed his rival.

Therefore, he restrained himself, and made friends with the rival instead.

At that moment, Genghis Khat's second favorite human (after Maggie, of course) arrived with her arms full of tasty morsels on plates.

"Can I get you anything, Jefferson?" Annie asked.

"He's just leaving," Jackson said, glaring at his brother.

"No, thanks, darling." Jefferson winked at Annie. "Gotta get back to work. Just stopped by to see my brother."

Right. Like anyone believed Jackson's brother was there to "see" him. *Torture* him was more like it.

"Well, let me know if you guys need anything else." Annie grinned and walked away, a slight spring in her step.

"I should be heading on." Jefferson climbed to his feet. "It was nice to meet you, Maggie, and you, Genghis Khat." Jefferson scratched the cat's head one last time, winked at Jackson's mate, then turned and sauntered out of the diner.

Jackson was only mildly appeased to notice that Maggie didn't once look Jefferson's way as he spoke to her nor did she turn to watch his retreat.

Instead she was focused on cutting her burger into what appeared to be four perfectly equal portions.

Annie, Jackson noticed, had set the can of tuna on *his* side of the table.

Jackson scowled.

Was he actually supposed to feed the cat himself?

At least it had a pop top, but still.

He glared at the can of tuna, then looked at his burger.

Damn cat could wait.

He reached for the burger, then jerked his hand back when the cat snapped at him with its teeth.

No. Not at him.

At his burger!

With one lunge, the demon cat managed to extract an

entire piece of bacon right from the middle of his burger, dislodging the top bun in the process.

"Hey! Why you little bacon thief!"

A spate of giggles from across the way drew Jackson's attention away from the cat and back to Maggie.

Her shoulders shook with laughter as she tried to get the bacon away from the demon cat. "Come on, now, Genghis Khat. Bacon isn't good for you. Too much salt."

The cat just growled low in his throat as he quickly gulped down the piece of bacon Maggie hadn't managed to pry from what Jackson was convinced were jaws of death, then turned his head to look speculatively at Jackson's burger.

"Oh, no, you don't." Jackson wrapped a protective arm around his plate and with the opposite hand, quickly set his burger back to rights and lifted it to his mouth where he took a giant bite.

Maggie giggled again.

Jackson had thought her beautiful from the first minute he saw her, but when she smiled, her eyes lit up and she was simply stunning.

"You should probably feed him some of that tuna," Maggie advised. "Then he won't be after your lunch."

Jackson scowled. "I notice he's not trying to steal *your* bacon."

"Of course not. Genghis Khat loves me, don't you, darling?" She kissed the cat on his forehead and crooned soft words to him as Jackson set about popping the top on the can of tuna.

"Here." He shoved the can across the table.

The demon cat gave it a dismissive look, then turned away.

"Seriously?"

Maggie snickered. "Oh, come on, Genghis Khat. It's perfectly good tuna."

In response, the cat actually put his nose up in the air.

"Fine," Jackson said. "I'll just enjoy the tuna myself then." He reached for the can.

In one swift move, the cat whirled and swat at him.

Jackson jerked back and let out a soft, rumbling growl.

Maggie jumped, startled, while the rest of the diner erupted in laughter.

Jackson scowled at the lot of them, then transferred his attention back to the cat.

The cat who had defended the tuna with a rather scary amount of viciousness, but who had not yet taken even the smallest of nibbles.

"Well, go on, then. You wanted it, eat it!"

Maggie shook her head. "You aren't doing it right. You have to feed him by hand."

"Excuse me?"

"It's why Annie brought the saucer. You have to scoop it out onto the saucer and then take a bit at a time and feed him."

"Are you seriously telling me that you hand–feed this monster cat like he's a baby?"

Maggie gasped. "He's not a monster, are you, Genghis Khat? And I only hand-feed him here at the diner."

Jackson groaned. "Great. Only here, where the entire town is witness."

Several snickers and chuckles rolled around the room, but he was too busy watching Maggie to pay them any mind.

She'd pulled the can toward her and was scooping the tuna onto the saucer. As he watched, she carefully divided the contents of the can into four equal parts, much like she'd done with her burger.

What followed was the strangest eating ritual Jackson had ever seen.

The cat, who had rejected the tuna from him, graciously accepted every tiny morsel Maggie offered. As she fed the cat, Maggie ate her burger. At first, Jackson thought it was his imagination, but no, as time passed, it became clear that Maggie was pacing her meal consumption right alongside the cat's. One-fourth of the burger and one-fourth of the tuna were consumed in approximately the same amount of time. She then went to work on the second-fourth of both.

Jackson couldn't decide if he was more disgusted or charmed. He really wanted to be disgusted, but he just couldn't find the process anything less than adorable.

Even though he still hated that damn cat.

He was so mesmerized by the process, he almost forgot to eat his own burger. For a while, the only sound at their table was Maggie murmuring soft words of encouragement and praise to the demon cat.

Jackson scowled. He wanted Maggie murmuring words of praise to him, damnit!

How ridiculous.

Jealous of a demon cat.

He wracked his brain for something to say to draw Maggie's attention back to him.

Wasn't there something he was supposed to be telling her?

Something important.

Oh. Right.

He cleared his throat. "So, Maggie, I wanted to talk to you a bit about *why* this town is so unusual."

Maggie glanced up from where she was feeding the cat another bite of tuna and said, "Oh. I didn't realize there was an actual reason for the strangeness." She looked disturbed for a moment. "You don't have to make up a reason for me. I'm perfectly fine with strangeness for its own sake."

Jackson didn't have the faintest clue how to respond to that. "Right. Well, there is a reason though and it's not one that I made up."

"Oh."

Damned if she didn't look *disappointed*.

"Well, I guess you'd better tell me then." She straightened in the booth, almost as if she was bracing herself.

"Okay, so it's like this. Everyone in this town is—"

"Maggie!" Livi slid into the booth beside Maggie and reached out a hand to pet Genghis Khat.

Unbelievable.

Jackson was beginning to think it was a conspiracy. He also couldn't help but notice that the cat didn't flinch or hiss or swat at *Livi*.

What *was* it with this cat?

He tolerated everyone but Jackson!

It was almost as if the cat *knew* Jackson had designs on Maggie, but that was preposterous. Right?

Jackson eyed the cat suspiciously.

Maybe it really *was* possessed by demons.

"You're coming to the party tomorrow, right?" Livi's question caught Jackson's attention.

Seriously? "Livi!"

"What?" She gave him an innocent look. "What on earth is taking you so long, Jackson Hewitt?"

Jackson glared at her and she only grinned unrepentantly back.

"Oh, I'm not much for parties," Maggie said.

"But you've never been to one of our parties," Livi said. "You'll love it!"

Maggie made a face. "Doubtful."

"I'm holding you responsible, Jackson," Livi said. "You get on with it right now and you bring her to the party tomorrow, you hear?" With that, she gave Maggie a quick peck on the cheek and was gone.

Jackson waited for Maggie to ask what Livi had been

talking about, but realized after a few moments that she wasn't going to ask. At first, he thought she was just being patient and waiting for him to share, but the more he studied her body language, the more he realized she just didn't care.

Livi had left and as far as Jackson could tell, Maggie had put Livi and the entire conversation out of her mind.

Maggie sat there, no tension in her body at all as she continued to croon to her ridiculous cat and feed him tuna, all while taking bites of her burger in between. She didn't rush either one. She never took a bite of her burger without first feeding the cat a bit of tuna and not once did she glance at Jackson for his reaction.

Lord, she was such a breath of fresh air.

How in the hell was he going to break the news to her about the town and him and that he was her mate?

Although, now that he thought about it, he was probably blowing everything out of proportion.

If he was lucky, she already knew about the town. After all, her mother and aunt had both been shifters, so none of this should be too big of a shock.

Right?

Ten

EVEN THOUGH THE humans in this town smelled wilder than most humans, Genghis Khat had begun to doubt Bygul's claim that some of them could change into animals.

In all their trips into town, Genghis Khat hadn't seen a single human shift, not even once, which was rather disappointing. It was also, in Genghis Khat's mind, pretty compelling evidence that Bygul had been sniffing too much of the catnip.

Then the sheriff went and ruined that theory by claiming he could shift into a panther.

Genghis Khat had never met a panther before, but he was pretty sure it was just a fancy name for cat.

Of course, until Genghis Khat saw the panther with his own eyes, he wasn't going to be falling for these ridiculous tales.

Maggie must have agreed with him because the next thing he knew she'd snatched him up off the table and was storming through the diner and out the door.

Genghis Khat smirked at the sheriff over her shoulder.

The last thing he saw before the door closed behind them was the sheriff lunging from the booth and running after them.

At least the idiot realized Maggie was *worth* chasing after.

MAGGIE COULDN'T BELIEVE IT!

The one man she'd kissed, the one man she really liked, was making fun of her. Just because her best friend was a cat whom she loved to talk to didn't mean she was gullible enough to believe people could actually change into animals.

There was *zero* scientific data to show that such a thing would ever be possible.

Jackson must believe she was an idiot.

It was the only explanation.

"Maggie, wait!"

She jerked open her car door and set Genghis Khat inside, then whirled to face Jackson. "Don't even say it."

He skidded to a stop in front of her. "Say what?"

"Whatever you're going to say. I don't want to hear it. I can't believe you think I'm so gullible as to fall for such a ridiculous tale. People shifting into animals. Oooh!" She was so angry, she couldn't even think of words to express how upset she was.

"I know this is a lot to take in, Maggie, but I promise you I'm not lying. I made the mistake of thinking you already knew about shifters, I'm sorry about that."

"Why would I know about—you know what? Forget it. It doesn't matter. I'm going home." She turned to open the car door.

"Because your mother was a shifter," he said quickly.

Maggie froze with her hand on the car door handle.

"Your aunt was too. They were both cougars. This town is mostly home to cougars, bears and wolves. Jefferson and I are the only panthers in town, and we're a bit of a scandal in the family, to be honest. There's this family legend, you see, about one of our ancestors, a wolf, having an affair with a panther. Nobody believed it, of course. It seemed preposterous, but then Jefferson and I were born."

Maggie didn't even know what to say.

Her brain was busy screaming, *but science,* while her heart really wanted to believe him.

It was a fabulous story and she was now imagining two panther cubs running around with a bunch of wolf cubs. It was a rather adorable image.

Dragging in a deep breath, she turned and said, "Fine. Then prove it to me."

"What?"

She waved a hand in the air and said, "Shift and show me your panther."

"I'm not saying no. I just can't do it here."

Maggie rolled her eyes.

"No, really. It's illegal to shift downtown. It's for the town's protection and since I'm the sheriff, I really kind of have to set the right example."

Maggie sighed. "Fine. Then where *can* you shift?"

"Pretty much anywhere else."

"My house?"

He smiled. "I'll follow you there."

Maggie didn't respond, just climbed into her car and pulled out of the parking space.

Deja vu filled her at the sight of Jackson standing in the parking lot, hands on hips, watching her drive away.

She couldn't believe she was even entertaining this possibility.

It was ridiculous.

Why she was catering to this madness, she had no idea.

She should have asked the others in the diner before leaving.

She probably could have proved he was lying right then.

After all, no one else had mentioned being able to shift into an animal.

Annie, Kate and Livi didn't mention it once, even though Maggie had spent an entire afternoon and evening hanging out with them. In fact, no one in the salon or the movie theater had mentioned it either. Mr. Wilson and his assistant didn't mention it when she was in his office signing papers.

Yet Jackson acted as if the entire town was made up of shifters.

If that was true and everyone in town believed they could change into animals, maybe they were having a mass hallucination.

She wasn't sure there was any scientific evidence that mass hallucinations were real, but that seemed a more viable possibility than believing shifters were.

She was pulling up the long driveway when she realized she'd invited someone whose sanity she now doubted back to her house.

What would happen if he couldn't shift and prove it to her, something she figured had a high likelihood of occurring?

Would he completely lose it?

Was she going to have to pretend that he'd shifted into a panther, just to keep him calm?

Maggie shook her head.

No way.

She'd spent her entire life telling the truth, even when it hurt. She wasn't about to start lying now.

When she got to the house, she scooped Genghis Khat into her arms and retreated to the porch.

She stood there, behind the railing and watched as Jackson approached. "That's far enough," she said when he was about ten feet from the front stairs. "Go ahead and shift now."

He cleared his throat. "I have to take my clothes off in order to shift."

Okay, that was unexpected.

Perhaps she should have realized clothes would get in the way of a shift, but since she didn't really believe he *could* shift, she hadn't thought that far ahead.

"Fine. Just hurry up."

She wanted to look away, but she also didn't want to turn her back on the potentially crazy man standing in her front yard, so she just watched as he stripped.

Good night, the man was hot.

He peeled his tee-shirt over his head, the muscles in his chest flexing as he revealed a thin trail of dark hair that disappeared into his jeans.

Maggie wasn't used to lusting after anyone. Mostly, she just ignored people, but there was no ignoring this man or the way he made her feel.

Dear heavens, it would be a sincere tragedy if he turned out to be insane.

She set Genghis Khat down on the porch.

It didn't seem right to be lusting after the man while holding the cat in her arms.

She slowly straightened back up, her eyes trained on Jackson's form the entire time.

He kicked off his boots, dropped his belt and unbuttoned his jeans.

The sound of his zipper sent a shiver of lust down her back and she couldn't have looked away if she tried.

He peeled his jeans away and she caught her breath at the first glimpse of his cock rising thick and long.

She could barely breathe, he was so boldly beautiful.

It was because she couldn't look away that she caught every second of the shift she'd completely forgotten was the reason he was stripping in the first place.

His whole body shuddered as he dropped to his hands and knees and *morphed* into a completely different being.

Maggie didn't even realize she was moving until she was in the yard, standing in front of him, one hand outstretched, stunned at the beauty of the wild animal in front of her.

Then, Genghis Khat attacked.

Eleven

ENGHIS KHAT GROWLED as the wild scent of the sheriff intensified, filling the air.

Then the sheriff became something else.

Genghis Khat had one moment to realize Bygul hadn't been sniffing too much catnip after all, then he panicked.

Not because the sheriff became a giant, predator cat.

Not even because the giant cat was on Genghis Khat's territory.

No. The reason he panicked was because Maggie left the porch and got entirely too close to the predator.

Genghis Khat let out a yowl, hurtled around Maggie and dived onto the intruder's back, claws fully extended.

One minute, Jackson was mesmerized by the sight of his mate, reaching out a hand as if to pet him, her eyes bright with a kind of joy he never expected.

The next minute, a demon had landed on his back.

Jackson howled as ten claws sank deep.

He tried to shake the cat from his back, but that just made it sink its claws in deeper.

Jackson crouched low to the ground, turned his head and aimed his loudest, most threatening growl at the demon on his back.

"Don't you growl at my cat," Maggie shouted, startling Jackson.

Why was she angry with *him*? He was the one getting clawed to death over here.

"You scared him!"

Seriously? Who was she kidding? The demon cat was growling louder than Jackson, for heaven's sake!

"You should have shifted differently so he wasn't so intimidated by you!"

That was just ridiculous. It's not like he had a thousand different ways to shift. Or that one way was more intimidating than another. If anyone should be intimidated, it was him! He had the demon cat's claws in his back.

"Just hold still," Maggie snapped, "and I'll get him loose. Poor Genghis Khat. It's okay, baby. The big, bad panther isn't going to hurt you, I promise."

Poor Genghis Khat, his ass!

Jackson held as still as possible, trying to ignore the

continuous growls from the demon cat while Maggie attempted to coax the cat's claws from Jackson's back.

Unfortunately, Genghis Khat didn't seem inclined to go anywhere and sank his claws in deeper.

Jackson let out another howl of pain and tried to shake the cat off again.

"Oh, stop being such a big baby!" Maggie smacked his shoulder, which seemed unjust in the extreme.

Jackson was the one with claws embedded in his back, and yet, he was the one getting smacked by his mate!

"It's okay, sweet pea," Maggie crooned to the damned cat. "I've got you. One minute and we'll get you away from the mean, old panther."

Jackson could feel her peeling the claws of one paw out of his back and it didn't exactly feel awesome. He growled low in his throat and tried not to move.

He let out a huff of relief when the claws of that first paw were completely extracted.

On to the second.

He held his body tense as Maggie slowly extracted the claws from a second paw, then began working on the cat's hind claws.

Jackson was just starting to think freedom was imminent when Jefferson arrived.

"Yo, brother—" Jefferson broke off, let out a bark of laughter and that was all it took.

The demon cat yowled, scrabbled at Jackson's back with his hind legs, causing *Jackson* to yowl, launched forward and landed on Jackson's neck and upper back this time, claws sinking deep once more.

The real issue, though, was when the demon cat leaned forward and chomped Jackson's ear.

Hard.

MAGGIE WASN'T EVEN SURE WHAT HAPPENED.

One minute she had Genghis Khat in her arms and was coaxing him to unclench his hind claws from the panther's rump area and the next Genghis Khat was hissing and yowling.

One minute he was mostly in her arms, the next he was attached to Jackson's neck, teeth firmly clamped on his ear.

One minute, both of them were right beside her, the next Jackson let out a yowl to wake the dead and took off running.

"No, Jackson!" Maggie shouted. She stamped her foot. "Stop catnapping Genghis Khat!"

It was too late though. Jackson had disappeared around the corner of the house.

The sound of laughter penetrated Maggie's fury. She whirled around and glared at Jefferson, who was rolling on the ground, roaring with laughter. "Jefferson, do something!" She kicked the bottom of his foot.

Jefferson choked back his laughter and climbed to his

feet. "Okay, okay, I'll do something." He pulled out his phone, tapped the screen a couple times, then held it up as Jackson came barreling around the house, Genghis Khat still attached to his neck and ear.

Jefferson turned his body so that he followed the two as they raced across the front lawn and back around the side of the house. He then turned the phone toward Maggie. "Maggie, sweet love, could you explain what's going on here?"

Maggie scowled. "Are you recording right now? Genghis Khat is traumatized and your brother's catnapped him. Again! Do something!" She waved an arm toward the side of the house where they had disappeared.

Jefferson obligingly swung the camera that way, then back to the other side of the house, just in time to capture Jackson barreling by a third time.

"Well, there you have it, residents of Greensboro. Our sheriff has been defeated by the Mighty Genghis Khat."

Maggie let out a growl of frustration.

"Aw, don't worry, sweet Maggie. Jackson'll get tired soon enough and then he'll bring Genghis Khat home." As he was saying this, Jefferson was on his phone, undoubtedly doing something stupid like sharing the damn video with everyone in town.

"We might as well sit and relax." Jefferson gestured toward her front porch. "Trust me. When Jackson gets going, it can take a while before he gets worn out."

Maggie sighed. "I don't care about Jackson. He's a

panther. I'm worried about Genghis Khat!" She stamped up the stairs onto the porch.

"Eh, he'll be fine. Watch when they come back around. You'll see."

So Maggie took a seat and this time, rather than panicking, tried to pay attention as they raced by.

It was hard to tell what with Jackson running so fast. "Was Genghis Khat still chewing on his ear?"

"Nope. Here." Jefferson held out his phone so she could watch their last circuit in slow motion. "See there?" He zoomed in so Maggie could see the look on Genghis Khat's face.

He *definitely* wasn't chewing Jackson's ear anymore.

In fact, it didn't look like his claws were embedded in the panther's skin either.

Instead, Genghis Khat was crouched low on Jackson's back, his front legs dangling down either side of the panther's neck. His fur was flying, ears flattened to his head, and if Maggie wasn't mistaken, he seemed to be *enjoying* himself.

She zoomed back out so she could Jackson's face.

He didn't look quite as happy as Genghis Khat.

Ha.

Served him right.

At that moment, cars started pulling up Maggie's drive. "What in the—" She stood and stared as people started pouring from the cars.

Jackson raced by again, Genghis Khat clinging to his neck.

"Ten bucks on the cat," Bud shouted as he walked by carting a long, collapsible table.

"Which cat?" someone called back.

"The house cat, of course," Bud said to a round of laughter.

Maggie watched, flabbergasted as more and more people called out their bets, good-naturedly debating whether the cat or the panther would come out the winner.

Jackson and Genghis Khat flew around the corner again and the crowd shouted encouragement as they raced by.

"Get him, Genghis Khat!"

"Show him who's boss, Genghis Khat!"

"Aw, you can't let a house cat get the better of ya, sheriff!"

"Would someone please just stop them?" Maggie exclaimed.

"Stop them? Now would we want to do that, lass?" someone asked. "This is hilarious. Tell me someone's got pictures."

"Oh, I've gotten a video every time he runs by," Jefferson said, "and plenty of pictures to boot. Y'all missed what started it. The cat had hold of Jackson's ear something fierce!"

Everyone laughed.

Maggie wrung her hands. Why wasn't anyone listening

to her? "I'm really worried about Genghis Khat. Someone needs to rescue him."

"Rescue the cat?" Bud asked with a roaring laugh. "Looks to me like Jackson's the one who needs rescuing."

Maggie scowled. "Jackson is ten times the size of Genghis Khat. He scared my baby and now he's refusing to shift back!"

"Aw, Maggie, don't worry," Jefferson said. "I told you. Jackson will get tired soon enough and he'll just stop running. Once he stops, the cat'll let go, you'll see."

At that moment, Jackson came around the corner again, only this time he was walking. He reached the base of the porch stairs and settled into a heap.

Maggie raced down them and fell to her knees beside Genghis Khat, who was still lying on Jackson's back, but seemed to be sound asleep. "Are you okay, baby? Genghis Khat?"

Genghis Khat opened his eyes and yawned.

Maggie scooped him into her arms. "Oh, I was so worried. Did the big, bad panther catnap you again?"

Genghis Khat nudged her on the chin.

She settled him against her chest and walked up the stairs and into the house.

GENGHIS KHAT WAS A LITTLE PUT OUT WHEN HE heard Maggie telling the sheriff *and* Handsome Hewitt that the sheriff had scared him.

He wasn't scared of that stupid sheriff.

He'd been trying to save Maggie from him.

Didn't she realize he was *brave*, not scared?

Of course, Maggie also called the sheriff a big baby, which Genghis Khat found to be both accurate *and* hilarious.

In fact, Genghis Khat's ride on the sheriff proved exactly who was the brave one and who was the baby. After all, Genghis Khat never fell off once, no matter how fast the sheriff ran, and now the sheriff was completely worn out, just like a baby in need of a nap.

Genghis Khat broke that panther in good.

Maggie must have recognized his bravery because when she carried Genghis Khat into the house after that exhilarating ride, she kept telling him that he was the bravest, strongest cat in the world.

Now *that* was more like it.

He had to be brave and strong if he was going to protect her from mutant human-panther sheriffs.

"Dude," Jefferson appeared at Jackson's side and stared down at him. "That was hilarious, but I'm not sure it helped your courtship of Maggie."

Jackson growled and climbed to his feet, slowly stretching upward into his human form. He stalked around Jefferson to his clothes that were still sitting in a pile in the middle of the front lawn and pulled them on, wincing as they settled against the multiple puncture marks along his back and shoulders.

What a nightmare that had been.

Stupid demon cat.

"I have no idea what I'm going to do now. Maggie's never going to forgive me for endangering her cat."

"Why *should* I forgive you?"

Jackson looked up.

Maggie stood on the porch, arms crossed. "You scared him and then you wouldn't shift back. If you'd just shifted back, he would have let you go."

Jackson sighed. "If I'd shifted back, I'm not sure what would have happened to his claws. They were buried in my panther form, Maggie. What if I shifted back and they got destroyed in the shift? He's not part of me, he doesn't shift with me. I couldn't take the chance."

"Oh." Maggie looked stunned. "I–I hadn't thought of that. I didn't know there was a risk like that. Thank you, I guess, but why run in the first place?"

"The first lap was just in response to the pain. It was instinct and that's all. The second lap was because I could sense the cat relaxing and thought if I kept running, he might be willing to jump down. The rest of the laps were because he was enjoying them."

Jefferson let out a hoot of laughter. "Told you! That cat is badass!" He whirled to face all the people in Maggie's lawn. "Let's get this party started!"

A bunch of cheers resounded in response.

"Wait. What's going on?" Maggie looked around, seeming to finally realize that her front and side yard was crowded with the entire town of Greensboro.

"The party's been moved to your place," Annie explained.

"What?" Maggie screeched.

"Oh, don't worry," Annie said. "We'll take care of everything for you. You don't have to do anything at all."

"But, but, I'm not a—I can't—parties aren't my thing," Maggie wailed.

Jackson chuckled and bounded up the porch steps to hug her. "Don't worry, babe." He wrapped his arms around her and swayed with her, back and forth. "The party will stay outside for the most part, so you can escape inside whenever you need to." He pulled away, settled his hands around the sides of her neck, and used his thumbs to tilt her chin up.

"Everything's going to be just fine." He leaned down and kissed her, then kissed her again, simply because he couldn't bear not to.

His mate was simply amazing, beautiful, everything he

could possibly want in a mate and he had no words for how incredibly grateful he was for this unexpected gift in his life.

He was determined to earn that gift, to be deserving of it.

She may have calmed down and even forgiven him for the fiasco with the cat, but he knew he was on thin ice.

One misstep and he could lose it all.

With this in mind, he focused on wooing his mate, giving her everything he thought she needed as the hours of the party wore on. He took her inside when the socializing became too much, ran interference for her when it was obvious she was done with the talking, danced with her when he thought she needed to be held and fed her whenever she seemed hungry.

Unfortunately, the entire town seemed to be in a conspiracy to constantly interfere with his efforts though.

Jefferson kept stealing Maggie away whenever someone distracted Jackson.

Then Jackson would be informed by some other townsperson that he'd better step up his game or his brother would end up stealing his mate.

It was a constant cycle of Jackson reclaiming his mate, dancing with her, wooing her, kissing her, stoking their passion, only to have Maggie stolen away when someone distracted him again.

Then there was the constant teasing and the paying of bets as videos of his panther and Genghis Khat flickered on the white screen off and on all night.

At first, Jackson was annoyed.

The videos were just a reminder of how worried Maggie had been about Genghis Khat, but somewhere in the middle of the fourth cycle of those damn videos, she finally saw the humor in the entire experience and actually started to giggle at the ridiculous pictures of the demon cat clinging to his panther.

He wasn't exactly thrilled that his brother had recorded the entire situation for posterity's sake, but he did love hearing Maggie laugh.

They spent the final hours of the party, dancing in each other's arms on the driveway, waving goodbye as one after the other of their friends headed off into the night.

Twelve

GENGHIS KHAT AND Bygul were stretched out on the porch, watching the party wind down.

"Pretty good party, G.K."

Genghis Khat had to agree.

He'd especially loved the part where they played pictures and videos of him attacking Baby Sheriff.

He'd looked so fierce while locked onto the panther's ear!

Everyone had cheered and laughed and congratulated Genghis Khat.

He'd been the hero of the event.

"Good treats too," Bygul said.

Those were thanks to Annie.

"Hm. Maybe I'll have to find this Annie a cat companion too," Bygul said.

Genghis Khat let out a small growl at the idea.

Annie might decide to feed the companion cat instead of Genghis Khat and he wouldn't like that at all.

Bygul stood and stretched. "Well, I'll let you get back to your human and her mate. Looks like things are progressing quite well there. Overall, really nice job with the mate-matching, G.K."

Then Bygul was gone.

Genghis Khat hadn't exactly enjoyed the whole mate-matching gig.

And he definitely didn't like the mate in question, but he did love Maggie so he'd keep trying to help, even though he knew Baby Sheriff wasn't anywhere near good enough for her.

THOUGH MAGGIE HAD ALWAYS HATED PARTIES, TO her surprise, she wasn't exactly hating this one. In fact, she found herself having fun as the night wore on.

Jackson was so attentive and sweet.

He always seemed to know when she needed a break and would sweep her into the house without ever seeming disappointed or annoyed. He was happy to just sit with her in whatever room she retreated to where she would listen to music and pet Genghis Khat, who *always* followed them inside.

Even if he'd been nowhere near them when they retreated, Genghis Khat always seemed to know when Maggie needed him and was always there within a few moments, nudging her hand and purring.

Those few moments when she retreated inside, cuddled Genghis Khat and just basked in the quiet seemed to rejuvenate her and gave her the energy to go back out and socialize a bit more.

Jackson followed her everywhere, catering to her every need.

Before she even realized she was thirsty, he was slipping a coke into her hand.

Hunger was just around the corner when he brought her a plate full of foods she loved.

When she was tired and needed to sit, he had a collapsible chair ready for her.

When she was feeling overwhelmed, he pulled her onto the driveway and into his arms and just swayed with her.

Those were her favorite moments.

Wrapped in Jackson's arms, feeling safe and cherished.

He took all the teasing good-naturedly, even when she stiffened at the memory of her worry when he'd first bolted with Genghis Khat clinging to his shoulders.

He even refrained from punching his brother, something he clearly wanted to do, given his glares every time Jefferson absconded with her.

She was fairly certain Jefferson was just messing with

him, which was why she'd asked him, "Why are you torturing your brother?"

Jefferson had just laughed. "He's just too easy and it's fun. Besides, believe me, your ma—uh—your man will get his revenge. He always does." He'd then spun her out on the driveway and danced with her a couple minutes before Jackson managed to get away and steal her back.

They made her laugh and she didn't think she'd ever really laughed before she met the two of them.

In the end, the party was magical and Jackson utterly charming.

When the evening finally ended, she was in Jackson's arms, swaying and kissing him.

The last of the shifters had left—she *still* had to process the fact that shifters were real and her mother had been one of them—and now Maggie was alone with the one she cared about the most.

He helped her with the last bit of clean-up—as Annie had promised, there really wasn't much left to do—then he kissed her good night (multiples times), before leaving her at the door with a promise to see her in the morning.

He was supposed to pick her up at eleven for a surprise.

He ended up seeing her much earlier than expected, however, when he woke to discover Genghis Khat hanging out in his bedroom.

He returned the cat to Maggie and they got an earlier start to the day than expected.

He took her on a picnic breakfast to one of the lakes in

the area and they spent the entire day getting to know each other better.

He told her about growing up as a panther among a family of wolves and about the mischief he and Jefferson got into around town. He told her about the tricks they used to play on their family, friends and neighbors and about one memorable double date when the twins switched places midway through.

"We thought we were so clever." Jackson laughed.

"Your dates didn't notice?" Maggie exclaimed incredulously.

Jackson shrugged. "Most people can't tell us apart, Maggie."

She rolled her eyes, then told him about growing up with parents who didn't understand their only child, about dropping out of school and getting her GED because school was a torture chamber from the first day in kindergarten and about the spiral notebook where she'd kept a list of all the jobs she'd worked through the years, sorting them into various categories like factory jobs, office jobs, service industry jobs and retail jobs.

Jackson scowled at the story of the employer who harassed her, cheered when she related how she'd knocked him out with one punch and laughed uproariously when she described her fear of the dead rising as zombies and devouring her at the morgue.

It was probably the most talking Maggie had ever done in her lifetime in one day. The most amazing part, though, was that Jackson didn't seem to mind when the conversation lapsed into silence. He seemed perfectly content to wait for Maggie to start up the conversation again.

It was crazy.

She'd only known him a couple days and she was already falling deep under his spell.

The following week passed in a blur of moments all strung together like precious diamonds—the picnic by the lake, cuddling and kissing on her couch while a movie played in the background, hiking in the woods, going for a hayride, endless meals at the diner—and every day with Jackson began, inevitably, with the catnapping of Genghis Khat.

Jackson swore up and down that he was not the one letting Genghis Khat out or transporting him to a new location every day, even though that new location was *always* where Jackson happened to be in that moment.

More and more, it seemed like Jackson's illogical theory of god magic was the only one that made sense.

It was a full week after the party that Jackson said to Maggie words he'd said once before, words that had changed her entire world view.

"Maggie, I have something to tell you."

Not again.

"What is it this time? Vampires are real?"

He chuckled. "That I don't know. I'd say no, but we exist, so maybe?"

She could totally deal with that answer because as far as she was concerned, there was *zero* scientific proof that vampires existed, and therefore, she considered that answer to be a no. "So what then?"

"It's about shifters. And us."

"What about us?"

Jackson led her to the sofa, where he sat down beside her, turned and faced her and with her hands in his, said, "Maggie, I think you're my mate." He shook his head. "No, that's not right. I *know* you're my mate."

"What does that mean? Your mate?" She was afraid to hope. Afraid to believe.

"Shifters only mate once and they do it for life. They usually know their mate from the minute they meet, though there have been times when mates knew each other from childhood and didn't realize it until well into adulthood. In our case, though, I knew the moment we met. You're my mate, Maggie."

"But what does that *mean*?"

"It means you're mine and I'm yours and I'm falling in love with you."

Maggie shook her head. "That's not even possible. You don't even know me. We've only known each other a week."

"Eleven days, to be exact."

"You can't count those first two days. We only talked on the phone for a couple minutes at most. And you were annoying."

Jackson chuckled. "Say what you will, I'm still counting them. Besides, we shifters don't need that much time. I've learned everything I need to know about you."

Maggie shook her head. "You're insane if you believe that's true. And even if it is, I'm not a good bet, Jackson."

"Of course, you are, Maggie. You're the best bet in the world, at least for me."

"You don't understand. I'm too weird. You'll get tired of me and then you'll leave me, so it's best we don't get our hopes up. So far, everything's great, but it won't last."

"You're not weird. You're perfect."

"I'm not polite. I'm too honest. I say things without really thinking about them and people's feelings get hurt or they get mad and they don't like me anymore. It'll happen eventually, even with you, Jackson."

"I love that about you."

"No—"

"Yes. Listen. I *love* that about you. I love that I know exactly where I stand with you, that you'll never pretend to be happy when you're not, that you'll never say you're fine when you're really hurting, that you'll never say something you think I want to hear rather than what you're really thinking. I *love* that about you."

"I'll ignore people when they want to talk to me, they'll complain to you and you'll find that annoying."

"I absolutely won't. I'll always be happy to run interference if you need me to, to get you away from any situation if that's what you need, whatever is necessary for your happiness, Maggie."

"You won't feel that way when *you're* the one I'm ignoring."

Jackson chuckled. "Part of being mates is understanding each other and giving each other what we need. If you're ignoring me, I'll know it's because you've hit the wall and it's *not* a good time. I will always take care of you, Maggie, even if that means waiting until you're ready to talk. *This* is what being mates means. I'm here for *you*. *You're* my number one priority, no one else, not even me."

She stared at him, trying to decide if she could trust that he would stay the course, that he wouldn't one day decide she was just too much work.

"Maggie. I'm falling in love with *you*. Not the idea of you, but *you*. Crazy, wonderful, you. Maggie who talks to her cat like he's a person who might respond at any minute. Maggie who shouts at me when she's angry, who doesn't hesitate to smack me, even when I'm in my panther form when she needs me to pay attention. Maggie who always says what she means and does exactly what she says she will. You're the one for me, Maggie. Not anyone else. *You*."

Maggie flung her arms around his neck and hugged him tight.

He pulled back, then kissed her.

She clutched his shirt and kissed him back.

Shivers raced up and down her spine as his tongue tangled with hers and a growl rumbled deep in his throat.

"Jackson," she whispered.

His hands clenched on her hips and he dragged her into his lap so she straddled him and held on.

They kissed and fumbled in the dark and kissed some more.

He put her from him when they were so breathless, she was gasping, and her whole body felt like it was going up in flames.

"You're mine, Maggie," he growled, "but we'll wait until you're feeling completely secure in this mating." He pulled her back into his arms for one last devastating kiss, then in a display of strength she found astonishing, surged to his feet and carried her to the door, kissing her the entire way there.

When he reached the door, he set her on her feet, kissed her one last time and murmured, "Lock the door behind me. I'll see you tomorrow, my love."

"Tomorrow," she whispered back, then watched as he stepped out onto the porch.

She closed and locked the door, then darted to the picture window in a ritual she'd been following since the first night he'd kissed her. She watched, as she had that night and every night since, as he sauntered down the walk, climbed into his car and drove away.

This time, when she picked up Genghis Khat, she wasn't shaking and she had no questions. Instead, she whispered in his ear a secret she'd been holding close to her heart. "Genghis Khat, you won't believe it, but I think I'm falling in love with that man."

Thirteen

GENGHIS KHAT DIDN'T exactly approve of Maggie falling in love with Baby Sheriff.

Nor did he approve of the romance that followed.

However, he did have to admit that Baby Sheriff was doing everything in his power to prove how important Maggie was to him.

He courted her and made it clear that she was the center of his world.

Genghis Khat still liked Handsome Hewitt more, especially since the man always brought him treats whenever he visited.

As a bonus, it made Baby Sheriff annoyed whenever he saw Genghis Khat scent-marking Handsome Hewitt.

Unfortunately, Bygul had insisted Handsome Hewitt

wasn't in the running for Maggie's mate, so Maggie and Genghis Khat were stuck with the sheriff instead, leaving poor Handsome Hewitt all alone.

In Genghis Khat's opinion, it wasn't exactly fair that the more deserving of the twins had no mate of his own.

Therefore, even though Genghis Khat had been looking forward to retiring his mate-matching skills, he decided to make one more match.

He'd need to recruit Bygul's help, of course.

After all, Bygul was the reason Genghis Khat was stuck with Baby Sheriff, so as far as he was concerned, Bygul owed him big.

Unfortunately, Bygul refused to even consider it without bringing in another cat, so Genghis Khat grudgingly agreed Bygul could recruit a companion cat for Handsome Hewitt as well.

As long as the new companion understood, of course, that Genghis Khat was in charge.

THE FOLLOWING MONTH WAS THE MOST wondrous of Maggie's life.

She'd found a home that was populated with people who didn't mind her strange habits or her unwillingness to talk at times.

They didn't mind when she was silent or when she was what other people had called "rude and unfriendly." They just accepted her and were kind to her.

Then there was Jackson.

Her mate.

He wooed her with kisses and sweet words and made her realize how incredibly lucky she was to have such a wonderful mate.

And somewhere, in the process of gaining friends, a town, a home and a mate, she also gained a big brother.

She'd never had any siblings before and found Jefferson to be everything she could have ever wanted. Protective and funny, sweet and charming, and as a bonus, he *never* said what he didn't mean.

Neither did Jackson or any of her friends in Greensboro, for that matter.

She'd eventually come to realize it was because shifters could somehow scent deception.

Even a well-intentioned lie had no chance of success among the shifters.

As far as Maggie was concerned, this was a dream come true. She'd finally found the perfect place for her.

The only annoyance was the continued catnappings that Jackson *still* insisted he was not responsible for.

Maggie wasn't sure she believed him since Genghis Khat kept disappearing from her house and reappearing wherever Jackson was.

Every day, at some point during the day, Jackson would text Maggie to let her know where Genghis Khat had shown up that day.

The sheriff's office.

The diner.

The library.

The bookstore.

The courthouse.

The mayor's office.

The town square.

By the time a month had passed, Maggie had been inside every public building in Greensboro and some private ones as well.

It was rather awkward when she had to pick up Genghis Khat from Jefferson's house.

Awkward because Jackson had gotten a call out and forgot to let Maggie know, so when she arrived to pick up Genghis Khat and found him in Jefferson's lap in the backyard, she'd come up behind Jefferson and had kissed him on the cheek before realizing he was the wrong twin.

She'd leapt away in horror while Jefferson had roared in laughter.

He'd then asked how she'd figured it out since most people couldn't tell the twins apart.

Maggie had just shrugged and said, "I don't know why people can't tell the difference. To me, it's obvious."

In truth, they were pretty damn identical. They even had

the same haircuts, but somehow Maggie could always tell them apart.

She'd known the second her lips had brushed Jefferson's cheek.

There was just no spark.

She should have realized it sooner, but she'd been too focused on sneaking up on him.

Cat hearing made that almost impossible, but she kept trying.

At some point, weeks into her relationship with Jackson, she realized she no longer worried that he would change his mind or that he would find her annoying.

In a month of spending almost every free minute together, he'd been treated to *all* of Maggie's idiosyncrasies and not once had he seemed impatient or angry.

He accepted when she needed quiet time.

He was fine when she didn't want to go outside or socialize.

He didn't even get upset when she ignored him for almost forty-eight hours that one time. She'd just retreated into her head for a while. She wasn't sure why. It just happened sometimes.

When she'd finally surfaced, she'd asked why he hadn't gotten upset with her and he'd told her that he could sense she was okay and nothing was wrong, so that was enough for him.

He'd still spent time with her each evening, not pushing for anything from her, and when he'd left, he'd brushed a kiss on her cheek and had admonished her to lock the door as usual, but that had been it.

That was when Maggie finally began to trust that Jackson would never let her down, that this mating was truly solid and would last a lifetime.

She waited another week, just to be sure.

Then, one Friday night, when they were making out on the sofa, as they did every night, Maggie whispered in Jackson's ear, "I want our mating to be real. I'm ready."

He pulled away and stared into her eyes. His were lit with joy, but still he asked, "Are you sure, Maggie?"

She nodded. "I'm positive."

He swept her back into his arms and kissed her.

Maggie thought she knew everything about Jackson's kisses by then.

How incredibly tender and sweet they could be and how devastatingly hot and passionate.

In that moment, though, she realized how much he'd been holding back.

He devoured her mouth, tongue tangling with hers, as he lifted her in his arms and carried her to her bedroom.

He laid her on the bed and followed her down, still kissing her, still driving her mad with passion.

"Jackson," she whimpered, clutching at his shoulders, trying to get closer, trying to find some relief from the unrelenting heat.

"Maggie," he murmured. He sat up, pulling her with him. He peeled his shirt off, then hers, then unhooked her bra and flung it away. He caught her breasts in his hands, tweaking both nipples and making her gasp.

She collapsed back onto the bed and he followed her down, capturing one nipple in his mouth while tweaking the other with his hand.

She writhed on the bed and gasped out his name. "Jackson, please." She grabbed the back of his head, clutching the hair there, holding him to her, but wanting, needing more. "Please, I need you."

He groaned, then jackknifed up and off the bed. "Should have stripped first," he muttered, struggling out of his jeans and boxers, only to get hung up at the boots.

He stumbled around the room, trying to kick them off, almost losing his balance in the process.

Maggie would have laughed, but she was frantically trying to get out of her own jeans without leaving the bed.

It didn't help that she couldn't pull her eyes away from Jackson.

Even hopping around the room with his jeans half-on and half-off, one boot on and one boot off, he was the sexiest man she'd ever seen.

She was so busy watching him that she forgot her own mission, so when he finally got free of his boots and jeans, he had zero patience for her own. He stripped them off her so fast she was once more in awe of his strength as he lifted her entire body with one hand while the other made short work of her jeans and panties.

He dropped her to the bed, settled his shoulders between

her legs, leaned forward and swiped his tongue through her folds.

Maggie gasped and fisted the sheets beneath her hands.

Jackson settled one arm across her belly, pinning her to the bed and with his other hand, opened her wide for another swipe of his tongue.

"Jackson!" she wailed. She couldn't escape his questing tongue, could only lie there and *feel*.

White sheeted across her vision as he caught her clit in his teeth and tugged gently.

For one long moment, she was frozen on a precipice and then she broke.

Everything clenched hard, then shattered.

The first sense that came back was her hearing.

The room still echoed with the sounds of her cries of ecstasy. Beneath that was her ragged breathing and a soft growling from Jackson.

She lifted her head and looked down her body to see that he was still between her legs, nuzzling her pussy, growling softly as he slowly licked it clean.

She whimpered at the sight. "Jackson."

He raised her head and looked at her. His eyes were wild, almost as feral as the panther's.

Her heart skipped a beat, then began pounding an impossible rhythm. "Jackson. I need you."

He let out another soft growl, then slowly prowled up her body until he reached her face. He settled one hand against her cheek and kissed her.

Slow. Gentle. Tender.

He settled over her, lodging his cock right at the entrance to her pussy, then waited.

She arched up slowly and begged, "Please, Jackson. Now. Please."

He reached down, grabbed one leg and pulled it up, then slowly began to penetrate.

Maggie's eyes fell shut at the sensation.

Jackson growled and her eyes flew open again, catching his.

Staring into his eyes, she could barely breathe as he slowly, so slowly, plowed forward, stretching her, claiming her, welding them together as one.

"Maggie," he growled. In that one word, she heard a wealth of passion and affection.

Finally, he was fully seated inside her. She could feel him everywhere, in every part of her being. He was hers and she was his.

"Jackson," she whispered.

He leaned down and growled, "Are you ready?"

"Yes. Yes, Jackson."

He pulled back and powered forward, the sensation so intense, Maggie whimpered and clutched at him tighter. "Please, Jackson. More."

As if that was all he needed to lose control, Jackson braced his arms on either side of her and let loose.

The friction, the incredible sensation of being filled with him, then empty, then filled again had Maggie crying out and begging for more.

She lost track of time and space. All she felt, all she knew was Jackson.

He was her everything.

When she broke this time, she didn't even know it was coming. It just came in a wave so powerful, it swept her under and it kept going and going and going.

"Jackson!" she shrieked.

He let out a growling roar and plunged deep.

Warmth bathed her pussy and another orgasm wrenched through her, causing everything inside to quake.

Jackson collapsed on top of her, then carefully rolled them both so that they were still connected, but she was on top.

For several long moments, they lay in each other's arms, gasping for breath and shuddering through the aftershocks of pleasure.

Into the silence, Jackson said, "God. *Damn.*"

Maggie giggled. "Is it always so..."

"Intense?"

"Yeah."

"Not in my experience, but I have a feeling you and I have just hit the tip of the iceberg when it comes to the intensity of our mating."

"We may not survive."

"Eh, maybe not, but what a way to go."

Maggie laughed, then lifted up to see his face. "Jackson?"

"Yeah, babe."

"I love you."

He rolled them so that she was on her back again and he was crouched over her. He settled his hands to either side of her neck, sliding his fingers into her hair so they cradled her head. "I love you too, my Maggie, my mate, my everything."

They got very little sleep that night as they spent it solidifying their mating, catching tiny catnaps between bouts of loving, only to rouse and love some more.

At some point in the wee hours of the morning, Maggie felt Genghis Khat jump onto the bed and smiled.

Her world was now complete.

GENGHIS KHAT WALKED ACROSS BABY SHERIFF'S stomach, flexing his claws and making the panther hiss, then curled up on Maggie's pillow.

Even though the sheriff had intruded on their space, Maggie didn't hesitate to cuddle Genghis Khat close and to whisper to him, as she did every evening, that he was the sweetest, best cat ever.

Baby Sheriff made a scoffing sound in the background, but Maggie slapped her hand over his mouth and snapped, "Knock it off, Jackson."

She then turned back to Genghis Khat and finished their ritual with a kiss on his nose and a whispered, "I love you so much, Genghis Khat."

Best. Human. Ever.

Read on for an excerpt from Jefferson's story
in The Real McCat.
It's going to be another Pawsitively Purrfect Match.

"For goodness sake, Maggie!" Jefferson bellowed. "Stop being so rude to the customers. You'll drive all my business away!"

Maggie glared at her brother-in-law. He had a lot of nerve, complaining about her customer service skills. "You do realize I'm only doing this as a favor because you're my mate's brother and he begged me to help you out. So really, I'm doing this as a favor to him, so he doesn't have to listen to you whine anymore."

"Yes, well, I had no idea this favor would involve you hanging up on my customers—"

"He was rude!"

"—insulting their vehicles—"

"It's ugly as sin!"

"—and refusing to answer the phone more than once an hour!"

"It rings entirely too often!"

"How is this any better than me not having a receptionist at all?"

"I don't recall promising it would be any better. In fact, I'm pretty sure I said I couldn't promise to be personable or friendly or even to do a good job."

"I thought you were joking!"

"Well, I wasn't. And frankly, if you don't want me to be rude to your customers, then you should recruit a better set of them. I have no idea why you can't just stick to customers from our own town."

Jefferson let out a furious growl, then spun around and stormed out of the office, probably back to the bay where he was working on some useless sports car. At the last moment, he yelled over his shoulder, "And stop painting your nails in my office. It reeks!"

Maggie grinned down at her nails. They were now a beautiful shade called Lucky Lavender and they were a perfect match to the flowers on her skirt. Who cared about scents when the result was this awesome?

She supposed she should feel bad about driving Jefferson crazy and about being rude to his customers and possibly losing him some money along the way, but really, she just didn't.

Because as far as she was concerned, none of this was her fault. In fact, she'd told both Jackson and Jefferson that they wouldn't like the results of her doing this favor for them, and they just hadn't listened.

Okay, so Jackson *had* warned her that Jefferson's shop was a ways out of town, at a crossroads between three different towns, and that one of those towns was full of humans, but that didn't mean Maggie had to like it.

She thought she'd left the whole customer service, dealing with strangers, human existence behind! Yet here she was, helping out her brother-in-law doing a job she didn't need and that she absolutely hated, just because her mate had asked.

This was what getting mated got you.

Fabulous sex, incredible friendships, romantic picnics, a big brother and *favors*.

A nudge on her arm ended Maggie's stewing. "Oh, Genghis Khat, you're so sweet." She leaned over and kissed the gray forehead of the best cat in the entire world. "Sorry for all the yelling, sweetie pie. And sorry we're stuck here in this ugly monstrosity of a building, instead of back at home in our awesome garden. Give it a few more days though. I may be his sister-in-law, but I guarantee Jefferson won't last much longer. He'll fire me before you know it."

"Um, excuse me?"

A woman stood in Maggie's office door, looking uncertain. She had short, black hair that kind of spiked outward in a really sassy way and was dressed in jeans and a tee-shirt.

"I saw the help wanted sign and—"

Maggie leapt to her feet. "Come in, come in. What's your name?"

"Kate Worcester."

"Nice to meet you, Kate. I'm Maggie. So, tell me what your qualifications are."

"Oh, well. I don't really have any. I mean, not as a mechanic anyway."

"Good because what we need is a receptionist."

"Oh, well, I don't exactly have receptionist experience either, but—"

"No problem." As far as Maggie was concerned, experience didn't really count for anything. After all, *she'd* worked as a receptionist plenty of times, but was absolutely *not* qualified for the job.

In fact, despite all her work experience, Maggie had *negative* qualifications, which meant that Kate, who probably had social skills, was higher than her on the qualifications ladder. "You're hired."

Kate's eyes widened. "Oh. Wow. Well, great. I mean—are you sure?"

"Absolutely! Okay, here's the deal. The phone rings and you answer it. Make appointments if they need one. Answer questions. If you don't know the answer, make something up."

Kate raised an eyebrow.

"Okay, no, probably don't do that. Just ask Jefferson. He's the boss."

"Um. Okay."

"I think that's it. Have a great rest of the day. The hours are eight to six, six days a week. You get Sundays off. If you need anything, well—just ask Jefferson." Maggie grabbed her bag, scooped Genghis Khat into her arms and headed for the door.

Kate swung around and followed her. "So what do I say when I answer the phones?"

"I usually just say whatever comes to mind. Usually hello. Sometimes car central or mechanics-r-us or whatever." Maggie wrestled the office door open and stepped through.

"Wait. Is that the name of the shop?"

Maggie threw a grin over her shoulder at Kate. "Nope. Never bothered to learn what it is. You could ask Jefferson that as well. He probably knows. Good luck!" With that, she let the office door swing shut behind her and bounced down the two steps leading into the garage.

Dropping a kiss onto Genghis Khat's head, Maggie giggled and whispered, "Let's go tell Jefferson the good news."

JEFFERSON FELT LIKE HE WAS LOSING HIS MIND AND might come unhinged at any moment. This was all Jackson's fault. He should have known not to trust his idiotic brother.

What a terrible idea, hiring Maggie as his temporary receptionist. What had he been thinking? He'd been desperate, true, but surely not *that* desperate? And now what was he going to do? Fire her?

Jackson would never forgive him.

Then again, if Jefferson was stuck with Maggie for the rest of his life, *he'd* never forgive Jackson.

"Jefferson, you're all set," Maggie called as she swept through the shop, Genghis Khat hanging over her shoulder.

Jefferson swung away from the car he was working on to glare at Maggie. "What's that supposed to mean? I'm all set for what?"

Was she leaving in the middle of the day? He didn't know whether to celebrate or mourn if that was the case. He had no one to cover the phones, but then Maggie barely covered them anyway, so it wouldn't be much of a loss.

"Your new hire's in your office, all ready to go."

"New hire? What new hire?"

"The receptionist I just hired for you." Maggie grinned at him as she walked out the bay doors and headed for her car, calling back over her shoulder, "You're welcome!"

Jefferson shuddered. What now?

Who could she possibly have hired in the fifteen minutes since he'd last spoken with her?

He stormed across the garage and bounded up the two stairs leading into the office, muttering, "I bet she hired some bum off the streets," as he slammed through the door.

Just inside the office, he stumbled to a halt, stunned at the sight of the woman sitting at his receptionist's desk.

"I assure you I am not a bum," the woman informed him.

Speechless, Jefferson just nodded, then turned and stormed back out of the office into the shop.

She'd hired a bear! And not just any bear, a freaking grizzly! And not just any grizzly, but Kate Worcester, of the ritzy, real estate Worcester grizzlies.

High maintenance, snooty as hell, full of themselves Worcesters.

Jefferson had never actually met Kate Worcester before, or really any of the Worcesters, but that didn't mean he didn't know about them.

Rich. Spoiled. Completely detached from their own roots. He doubted a single Worcester had ever run through the woods in grizzly form, let alone shit in them.

And Kate Worcester was supposed to answer his phones?

What the freaking hell?

Well, that went well. Kate rolled her eyes.

If that was Jefferson, she was probably in trouble.

A search through the paperwork on the desk had turned up a number of invoices with JH Automotive at the top, so she had at least one question answered.

There were so many others, though.

Like why she was working there in the first place.

Sure she'd walked in and asked for the job, but that was beside the point. She'd just been so angry and then she'd seen the sign. It had seemed like a message from the gods.

But now that she had a minute to think about it, she was

realizing there was no way she could do this job *and* everything else. On the other hand—

At that moment, her cell phone began to ring.

Great.

She considered ignoring it, but no. He'd just do something really obnoxious, like invade her privacy and track her down.

With a sigh, she dragged out her phone and connected it, but didn't say anything.

"Well?" Mason bellowed after a few seconds.

Kate swallowed a giggle. "What? You called me."

"So you don't even bother saying hello anymore?"

"It seemed unnecessary."

"Unne—whatever. Where are you?"

"Oh, didn't you get my note?"

"You couldn't possibly be referring to this ridiculous post-it note that says 'I quit,' now could you? I know that can't be right because my sister would never walk out on the family business that way." Mason's voice rose as he spoke until he finished with a very bear-like roar.

Kate raised an eyebrow. "I don't see why not. I made it very clear, Mason, that one of these days you would go too far. Well, that day is today!"

"Oh, come on, Kate, it wasn't that bad."

"You threw the alpha of the McDonald clan out the window! Of a two-story building!"

"Eh, I'm sure he landed on his feet."

"That's not the point. And they're wolves not cats!"

"He was flirting with you."

"He was negotiating to buy the Wheeler property!"

"Oh."

"I was this close to offloading those acres, then you came along and ruined everything."

"Well, that'll teach him to keep his distance when negotiating."

"Oh, please."

"So when are you coming back?"

"What do you not understand about the words, 'I quit'?"

"You can't quit, Kate. You're not a quitter. Besides, we need you."

"Well, I'm sorry, but I've already got another job."

"You what?"

"I've given my word and have already started, and you're right. I'm not a quitter. There's no way I could leave them in the lurch, now is there? Not after they've gone to all the trouble of hiring and training me." Kate hit the mute button so he wouldn't hear her snickering.

"Training—you only left the building an hour ago!"

Kate cleared her throat to get rid of any telltale amusement and hit the mute button again. "Who said anything about the training happening today?"

Mason let out a growl. "You're making this up, aren't you? You couldn't possibly have found a job and been trained in the hour since I last saw you."

"I certainly am not making this up. I'm the new receptionist at JH Automotive."

"Receptionist? Now I know you're joking! There's no way you'd take a measly—hold on a minute. JH—are you talking about Jefferson Hewitt?"

"I believe that's my new boss's name, yes."

Dead silence, then, "You went to work for the panthers?" Mason roared.

Start reading The Real McCat today.

Other Books by Pepper

THE MURRYSVILLE COALITION

The Crazy Cheetah Lady

One Sad Kitty

A PAWSITIVELY PURRFECT MATCH

Catnapped

The Real McCat

Unbearably Cute

A Catmas to Remember

This Cat's for You

Santa Kitty

Hocus Purrcus

Tridents & Tails

Abra-Cat-Abra

Satan's Kitty

Valen-Cats

Vampurr Lovin'

A Beautiful Cat-ship

Grave Cattitude

THE SHENANIGANS SERIES

Shifter Shenanigans

Witchy Shenanigans

Full Moon Shenanigans

Hotel Shenanigans

Dragon Shenanigans

Undercover Shenanigans

Spooky Shenanigans

Holiday Shenanigans

Valentine Shenanigans

Lucky Shenanigans

STORIES OF THE VEIL

Guardians of the Veil

Astra

Glory

Luna

Zara

Lotus

WICKED

No Rest for the Wicked

Wicked Is As Wicked Does

PAWSITIVELY PURRFECT TRILOGIES

THE CAT'S MEOW

Catnapped | The Real McCat | Unbearably Cute

HOLLY JOLLY PAWLIDAY

A Catmas to Remember | This Cat's for You | Santa Kitty

SHENANIGANS ANTHOLOGIES

CRAZED

Books 1-3

AMAZED

Books 4-6

HOLIDAZED

Books 7-10

SHENANIGANS

The Complete Collection

STORIES OF THE VEIL

THE UNVEILED

Astra | Glory

THE VEILED

Luna | Zara

WICKED DUET

WICKED

No Rest for the Wicked | Wicked Is As Wicked Does

About the Author

WWW.PEPPERMCGRAW.COM

PEPPER MCGRAW is a USA Today Bestselling Author of paranormal romance. Her life to date has sadly been paranormal-free, but she knows it's simply a matter of time before her fated mate finally appears. Until that glorious day arrives, she keeps herself busy writing (and reading) paranormal romances.

Pepper loves animals, especially cats, and spends her free time volunteering at local shelters and for Trap-Neuter-Release programs. She's had the supreme honor of winning occasional head butts and meows from the local ferals in her neighborhood and has even convinced a few to come inside and adopt her as their own.

BB bookbub.com/authors/pepper-mcgraw

f facebook.com/ShenanigansSeries

g goodreads.com/peppermcgraw

instagram.com/peppermcgraw_author

tiktok.com/@peppermcgraw

twitter.com/peppermcgraw

www.ingramcontent.com/pod-product-compliance
Lightning Source LLC
Chambersburg PA
CBHW040532170726
48295CB00012B/435